PAWN

ORLA KELLY PUBLISHING

D.S. Cash

Orla Kelly Publishing,
27 Kilbrody,
Mount Oval,
Rochestown,
Cork,
Ireland.

Contents

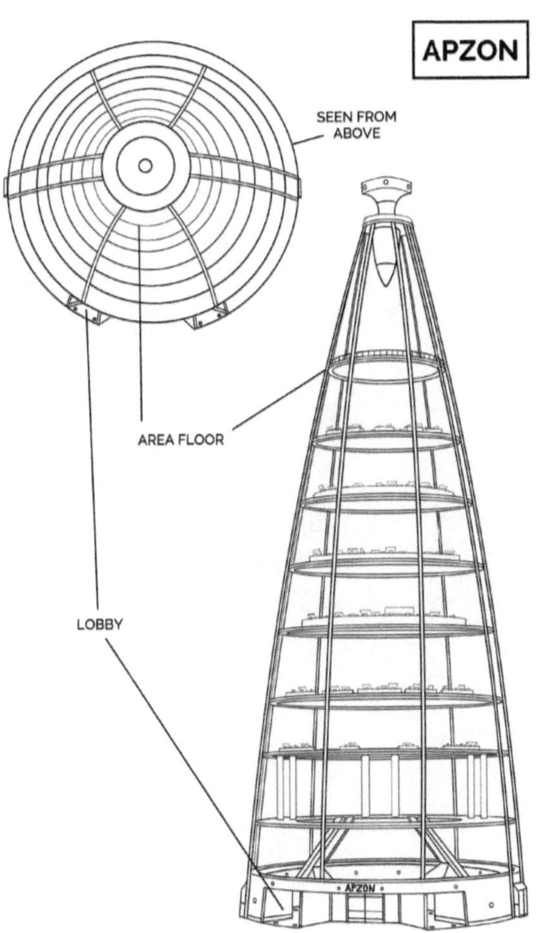
APZON
SEEN FROM ABOVE
AREA FLOOR
LOBBY
APZON

Chapter 1

A Good Opening Game is Important

Reader, see now the sand stretching from our toes to the horizon in the distance. Sand, sand and more sand, east to west, unable to escape the desert sun overhead.

Now a 'thud' sound. Something lands in the softness of the ground nearby. Then in quick concession, a hop-tap-tap sound.

Thud-hop-tap-tap.

Just like that, a golf ball rolls into view. This circle of the desert is littered with these balls: some here years and some just arriving. Golf is just one of the games people play here, but where are these people?

Beside the white dimpled ball, a hoof stomps into the sand. Then the animal's foot is gone as quickly as the other three feet that chase it. The camel they belong to is making a run for it, running across the sand towards the sun, sitting low out in space beyond the horizon.

Another camel. Then another. You know the type, the ones with one hump, not two. How many humps they have does not matter. But quickly, many of these desert horses appear from behind the cracked abattoir wall. A crazy man in his crazy car has forced a hole straight through the compound's perimeter wall, breaking its ring of protection and tearing open the abattoir's adjacent wall. The camels are running off into the outer desert. Chasing or following or doing whatever they are doing. I don't know. But they are running from something or towards something. Running for that line at the meeting of sand and space, yet running in different directions.

Many more camels are still inside the abattoir, waiting to make a run for it, queuing at this new hole in their wall. It doesn't matter how many humps the camels have; nor does it matter how many camels there are, because only one camel matters to us.

This one has made it outside but is not running out into the desert for its chance at freedom. This one camel is walking as if out for a casual stroll. Only short of lighting a cigarette, this one. Lumpy – that's its name – is looking back at the perimeter wall more closely.

Another wall? he thinks. *In the middle of the desert? And not a metaphorical wall, a literal wall. Of all the places to build a wall amid all these walls.*

Lumpy has always been too short to see what has been over the abattoir wall. The hole in the wall offers freedom from slaughter and his first opportunity to see what is beyond. Lumpy is having a good day. He looks through the crumbling eye in the concrete between him and the crumpled Mustang. The cut is wide enough for him to fit.

Should he go right with all the other camels into the desert and live the happy camel life he was born for? Or should he take a chance and go left? Choose left and go inside the wall that the 30-feet high perimeter wall has, all this time, *perimetered*?

Choices.

He certainly is not going back into the abattoir, the slaughterhouse. He doesn't much fancy being diced into cubes. He heads for Utopia. He's having the best of times, still years and miles away from the Winston and Max we know.

But getting closer.

—

Winston steps out of his cave-like home. It is near impossible to understand a cave from inside the cave. To understand something, anything, the best position is outside looking in. And what does that say about ourselves? It is probably not you who knows you best, but those around you, looking in.

Feeling stiffness in his ageing bones, Winston looks up at the morning sun. Is it morning? Under the desert sun, there is light and dark. Time is hard to track. He didn't think to bring a watch from home to this place and regrets that now most days. His watch sits miles away on a bedside locker in a house he hasn't stepped foot in years.

He doesn't want to think about it now as again he feels the heat of the inescapable sun in this place. He allows himself to remember rain for just a moment.

Is this a new day at all? he wonders.

They are all the same. Same, same, same, same. Blue sky, forest, mountains and lake, always the same and always painted in hot sunshine. But Winston remembers rain and can almost taste it this time. How many years has it been without rain? He is getting old here. He is having the worst of times.

Max has never seen rain. Nor rainbows. Nor either side of one. He doesn't yet know how to wish for over the rainbow or life in faraway places. He only knows the meta box they call home and the world of his grandad's story pages.

His little legs run him out to the door of that same homely bunker behind his grandad. Like Dorothy, red shoes carry him; little red trainers that belonged to someone else one time. Someone who Max will never know. They've been too small for Max for some time now. Grandad intends to find some new trainers when he goes to the city again.

Max is waving a red journal and calling out from the door of their cavernous steel hole.

'Wait, Grandad!'

Winston feels angry at the boy for getting so close to the door. *All energy, no thought,* he thinks. 'What are you doing? Not outside. You know this!' He looks into the boy's eyes and calms himself. He forgives the boy, recalling that enthusiasm once inside himself.

'You are forgetting,' Max says as he removes some blank pages from the back of the red journal he has been waving.

'Silly me,' says Winston, taking the papers and folding them. 'But I have paper I could have written on, you know?'

Max frowns. 'You didn't pack any. I checked your bag. Do they have blank paper at the post box? Can I come with you and see? Someday? Today? I know you said no, but I'm big now. I'm…'

'I know. I know you are,' Winston says, hurting in his chest. 'But it's dangerous, you know. I've told you.'

Max's head slumps, but the old man lifts his chin with a gentle forefinger.

'Hey, you're not technically thirteen until tonight, you know. Maybe tomorrow. Now get back inside in case someone sees you.'

The lunacy of that statement is not lost on Winston. There hasn't been a single other person passing through these trees in years. Still, he keeps the boy inside. He remains cautious.

We outgrow our boxes with time. Winston has always known he cannot keep his grandson squared in forever, regardless of the consequences of opening that box.

But Max is elated at the thoughts of going with Grandad to the post box. Grandad goes there every day to transcribe the words sent in code by Max's mother.

Winston smiles, tucking the pages into a pack.

'Wave me off ... from the door,' he says, kissing the top of Max's head. 'But stay inside.'

'I will.'

'I'll try to be home before dark,' Winston says, fiddling his arm through the strap on the backpack. 'Happy birthday, kiddo.'

He adjusts his cap's rim, and with a nod, Winston turns and walks into the wet forest as it glistens in the sun.

Chapter 2

The Bunker

Following Grandad's instructions, Max returns to the bunker. The bunker, though smaller than the others, has proved the perfect size for the two of them. The size was not the reason Winston originally chose this one. It was selected for its location.

Max likes the company of friends. So, every day, when Grandad leaves, Max fills the small bunker with characters from the stories. Being imaginary, they don't take up much space and eat nothing at all. The words and the characters on the pages are his only friends. Lives and deaths, lessons and morals on every page.

He has read the words many times over. Still, he is not tired of a single letter. Twenty-six letters, A, B, C, same, same, same. Yet, he is amazed that the few letters can tell so many different tales. The same letters can be new every day. Max can live a life amongst the words, knowing them each and all.

Thoughts of what stories Grandad will bring back excite Max. What will the new tales bring? What new characters to befriend? Max has only learnt or experienced new things with pages in his hands. He has collected all the pages, the separate stories within one cover, one book, one journal.

Even without that book, he can close his eyes and from memory, let the words float by in the darkness. By reading, he travels through other worlds and lives many different lives. Max likes it when Grandad reads to him as he falls asleep. He hears just enough to enter that world and create his own ending in dreams. He likes to fall to sleep right where the bait glistens in front of the heroes' eyes.

He likes beginnings because beginnings are safe. Beginnings are before the characters' worlds are forced to change. He is reading Mockingbird again and all about Jem and her friend called Scout. Max has always longed for a friend. He stops at the sound of something outside the door. He hears that voice – one that is young, not Grandad's.

Max twists the wheel, again and again, pushing the door out from inside. The door feels solid and heavy to his small arms, but its steel moves slowly under his push. He pokes his head outside, still clinging to the metal door frame with both hands. Again, he hears the voice. He has listened to the same voice for months now – always when Grandad leaves. He has been hearing it more and more in recent days.

The lake's surface is still, as usual. It looks calm, safe, only ten feet from the entrance of their bunker. Might he chance to go that far? Might that be far enough to find the owner of the voice?

The blue in his eyes begins to grow as the black of his pupil constricts. His virgin skin feels the sun's powerful heat, making Max inch back inside the bunker. For just a second, a face flashes between the leaves of the trees across the lake. Max is startled, and then the face is gone again.

The lake's edge now tempts Max even more. He pokes his head out again and sees another someone. But Max feels no instinct to hide. The person's back is almost entirely turned, but he can see she's a child, sitting upon a rock at the lake as if she has been there all her life. She sits kicking her feet in the water.

He steps forward, and her head swivels to the noise behind her. Max realises he is seen, and he is standing outside. Frozen, he stands staring at the little girl by the lake. At the little girl staring back at him. At Jem.

It's Jem from Grandad's story pages. He knows she ... well, actually, he is beginning to question what he knows. His eyes are telling different truths to Grandad's.

But Jem looks away now, rolls her dungarees higher – above the knee now – and makes more circles with her feet submerged in the water.

Max moves closer until he can sit on a large rock beside her. He removes his shabby shoes in the heat. In the daylight, he sees just how worn they have become. The shoes, once bright red, are faded. Resting the book on his knees, he flicks the pages. He is excited at each glimpse of a page filled with old friends and foes. The girl watches.

A noise startles Max, and he draws his legs close in fright as his eyes settle on a strange creature. 'Coo!' it says. *What is that?* He has never seen anything like it. Grey and moving as if it is alive, this thing watches him. It flutters onto the rock beside him. In a forest with no creatures and no people, Max sits with a young girl and a pigeon. Max has no idea what it is. All he knows are his eyes are telling different truths to Grandad's words.

With slender fingers, the girl reaches and tugs at one of the pages in Max's journal and pulls it free. Carefully watching Max, she slowly tears the page a little. Max snatches the book and its other pages out of her reach as she examines the leaf she has. The words seem to be invisible to her. She twists the page over and back, searching for the attraction that Max finds in it.

Of course, she cannot know her own origin. She cannot see it; cannot read it.

Max flicks the pages of his book. For a single moment, everything flickers. The world turns, and life within the pages revolves around Max, Jem and the pigeon. Max's attention is on the words while Jem and the pigeon look on at their interwound lives appearing in scenes that blink around the lakeside like the flickering of a film reel.

Pap-pap-pap. The bulb behind some invisible camera blinks. The pages flicker past Max's eyes until there are no more. Max counts 101.

He glances for the page that Jem has pulled free and sees the pigeon pecking it, shredding it into smaller speckles of paper; confetti-ing the page onto the bare rock.

Max snatches one piece, then two, careful not to touch that thing. Although the pigeon has not been a threat, Max is still cautious. He scrambles, gathering up every pecked paper piece. The book is all he has of her.

Max moves away from the pigeon. The bird looks back across the sun-warmed rock at the boy as he places the book before him and sprinkles the paper confetti on top. With the tips of his index fingers, he slides the pieces together until each paper disc is in its correct position.

He thinks.

It's a game. He has just remembered it. Or invented it. Which doesn't matter, but he is certain of it. Rook, knight, bishop, queen, king, bishop, knight, rook, fronted by a row of pawns. It's a game. He's sure it is, but where does it come from? How is it in his head?

He straightens up. Pleased with himself, he looks towards Jem. But she's gone. In her place, on the rock, is a strange man – the face from the trees.

—

Winston walks the well-worn track to his daily dig. The dirt along the route knows Winston's soul as well as it knows his sole. He stays close to the foot of the mountain, always under cover of trees; his boots treading the muddy pathway.

He follows the reservoir around the curve of the overshadowing rock and continues along the waterside. It takes two hours in total. However, he is close now.

He knows it as soon as he glimpses the Citadel appearing above the trees ahead. The green cone of the Citadel looks no different from anywhere you stand in this entire place. But he knows from habit when he has circumnavigated it.

Ten storeys high, the smart-glass, cylindrical building narrows until it reaches its pointed tip, a chimney-like opening on top. The trees and U City's other buildings rise to conceal the Citadel's lower levels from here. Winston can see the top four floors or so towering above the trees. And, of course, he can smell the Citadel's chimney. Winston checks around him habitually, even though he knows this forest is empty. He has reached the spot. He swings the pack off his back, flings it to the forest floor and removes the pages Max gave him from the front pocket.

The tree by his right shoulder is painted with a red 'X'. Max turns thirteen today, and for a long time, Winston has known what story he'll tell the boy this year. He knows the bond between parent and child is unique as he folds the pages and stuffs them into his rear pocket. Surrounded by forest, miles from the nearest human, he knows he has a lot of work to do. And on top of that, he has to remember the words.

—

Max is absorbed by words and characters and shakes his head. The man is no ordinary man. The sun reflects off the top of his coned head. He's losing. Max cannot remember what this game is called or how he knows it, but he proves good at it. The man's metal limbs squeak at his joints. The Tin-man never hides the fact that he has no heart. But often, Max questions the whereabouts of the Tin-man's brain.

A knight on horseback cuts across the water's surface in a gallop, the steed's heavy hooves thrashing violently through the water. The knight and horse swerve at the last second as they pass Max and the Tin-man. Max reacts with joy at the wave they splash over his and the Tin-man's heads.

Max rubs his eyes, blinded briefly by a sun flash reflected from a sword. A bishop waves shining steel before him. Max sees it clash with another blade in the hands of a darker dressed bishop. Out on the water's surface, the swords duel as the white king and white queen survey all from the shore, seated upon their thrones.

Ruby-red shoes and bishops of stone. Witches and wizards and king on a throne. Lions and Count of Monte Cristo's tower built on sand and treasures of gold ...

'Coo,' says the pigeon. And mockingbirds ...

As the warm, vibrating hum from the bird quietens, Max realises it is just him and the pigeon. Gone. Everyone. Again.

Stupid ... thing, Max thinks, looking at the pigeon. *Stupid grey ... thing.*

The pigeon hasn't vanished with the others. The knights and bishops and kings and queens. Why has it remained when reality returns? The pigeon has been there before the others too. Max extends a finger and leans towards the feathered thing, but it pecks sharply on his hand.

'Ow!' Max leaps back, nursing his hand. He's only distracted by movement in the tree line further up the lake. He watches, looking up through the silence of the vast valley, safely distant.

—

Grandad packs up to head back home. Enough tunnelling this day. He stops to open a box of bullets on the table. *Two or three?* he questions, knowing he only needs two. But should he bring an extra? Winston takes three. One for the boy, one for himself and one *just in case.*

—

Where did Jem go? Max feels alone. From behind a tree further up and across the lake, something large pokes its head out and disappears again. The trees rustle with an angry tussle, and the sound of grunting echoes down the valley.

Where has the girl gone? Has she gone back to her friend, Scout? Gone back within the pages of the book, back into Mockingbird? Max looks about.

'Where are you?' he whispers, wanting his friend. She has left with the others. His only friend his age is gone. Again.

The pigeon has not left. Nor has that monstrous thing across in the cover of the trees. Max sees the full size of his vast hulking form up-lake by the water's edge. Max can feel it. Something in the air or inside himself tells Max he knows that man. He has never seen him before, but he knows him. He's there in his mind like déjà vu.

—

Winston thinks he has remembered the words. He has done as best he can, at least. Re-emerging from the ground, he finds his shadow has spun around and grown longer since his time below.

Bent on one knee under the tree marked with the red X, Winston straightens the items inside the pack. He positions the bottle to stand up and not spill. A left and right shoe already is parcelled up and stuffed in with the pages he has written. He wedges a bottle of whiskey between them. Finally, he wraps his whittled gifts in a small square of cloth and shoves them in the pack. Grandad rolls the three bullets back and forth on his palm and seals them in his fist. He flips the bag's cover and then fastens the buckle.

Muck-filthy, from his elbows to his fingertips, Winston picks the rifle off the forest floor. He uses its butt to get back to his feet. The bottle swishes in the bag behind him as he pushes the three bullets into his pocket.

Winston takes a moment's breath, happy to be back in the open air. Then he starts for home. The route back is different as he passes where the daffodils grow. He never forgets to visit where his daughter lies.

The incoming cold of the night chases him home faster than the sun had chased him there. The open rifle is loaded and tucked under Winston's arm. Winston navigates the way from his daughter's resting place to the carved stone to home.

—

At the other end of the forest, Max's shadow has moved just as Grandad's has. Though the time passing has felt quicker to Max. As the last of the sun flickers on the lake, the small grey creature reappears, landing on a rock beside him in a flutter. It coos.

Max can hear this thing, this little grey-winged creature 'purring' from within its small chest. He stares at it. The bird tilts its feathered head to one side. And in the distance behind it, is the hulking man. Then he sees what the monster is watching. It's Jem. The girl plays by the lake, unaware of the monster's presence behind her.

The tiny girl, Max's first friend, his only friend, steps out knee-height in the water. It, the monstrous It, stays behind her. As she bends to touch the surface, It reaches out. In the distant quiet, Max watches this silent moment breathlessly.

This monster's blurred, plasticine-like face grows closer, and the small girl now senses it behind her. Max knows Jem feels the danger and wants the safety of her book's cover. She wants to go home and be wrapped back in the cover of To Kill a Mockingbird. She turns, and the creature's lips stretch in a cold smile. It proffers a daisy in its massive, outstretched hand.

The pigeon coos, but Max still stares as the girl's tiny hand reaches closer to the flower in the pale grey hand. Max rises to his feet. He knows this tale. He remembers it as if he has read it before.

As Jem's hand is within reach of Dr Frankenstein's monster, Max feels his insides quiver. Max runs up the lake towards Jem. He has never run this fast, this far, this free. He sees her as she takes the flower from the creature's offering hand and sees its other hand enveloping Jem's entire arm in his palm.

Max runs along the opposite lakeshore, watching as the monster plucks the girl up into its arms, ever so gently. Without any resistance, it drapes her across its bloodless arms. Then the creature begins to walk into the water holding the girl in its arms. It stares into her eyes as its steps ripple the water beneath her. Its eyes are fixed on the girl, not at the water's surface, not at its footing on the rocks beneath the water, not at Max across the lake from them. It watches the girl. Its eyes are firmly on those of the little girl in his arms. It watches her breathe.

Max runs and runs, struggling for breath. The water touches Jem's feet, and the child begins kicking, but the monster grips tighter to the struggling child. Then she is gone. She is below the surface, and Max hears nothing. The monster's eyes remain wide open as it sinks below the water, following its prey. Max reaches the opposite shore, right across from where the two have entered the water. He kicks his way in, desperately splashing water in every direction, hoping he is not too late. He swims out to where the monster was last visible. Splashing and swimming and more splashing, Max reaches down. He can get to Jem before her air runs out. Max's palms touch something below the water's surface. He grabs her. She is in his hands. He feels her kicking, trying to free herself from the monster's grip.

She wriggles, struggles, and he holds on. And then ... nothing. He can feel nothing in the empty lake. Nothing in his hands, nothing in the water. Nothing. Max looks back where he was sitting, back towards the bunker, towards the pigeon and home. Gone. There is no pigeon.

Max stands in the water, questioning the existence of a monster, questioning the existence of a pigeon. But he's distracted by a smell: a type of rotting stench that he feels churn inside himself. His pores taste this smell. His whole body is repulsed by it.

Something in every person's gene line makes this smell hard to stomach. A smell that alludes to a past Max does not know of, in a place miles from him and across waters he'll never know. A smell from a place Max has never been, and one he doesn't recognise. It's the smell of human flesh burning.

Then there's noise. *Tis, tis, tis, tis, tis, tis, tis.* It is coming from the trees nearby. Water sprays out through the trees from deep in the forest. Max now realises he has run far upstream. Now hundreds of yards from home, he is the furthest he has ever been. Looking around, he prepares for the forewarned danger. He has to stay indoors. Where is it? What is the thing he has spent his life hiding from? Maybe it is waiting to surprise him.

He sees a distant green spike in a gap between the trees – a tip of a cone-shaped building. This building's existence contradicts everything Max knows. It is large and glowing in the dimming evening light. Is that where Grandad goes? Max never expected the post-box to be so big.

Tis, tis, tis, tis, tis. The spray of water leaves the trees and waves across the lake. It splashes Max's face as it circles past him, and with it comes the smell. The sprinkled water runs down his upper lip and thickens as a flaky, dusty residue. He tastes it for the first time. Rotten.

He sees ash residue left on everything the sprinkler water touches. Tree trunks, leaves and branches are covered in stinking flakes of black and white slime. Still waist-deep in the lake, Max watches as a flake of ash floats in the air and sinks to rest on his forearm. The flake melts into his wet skin and turns it chalky black.

More airborne speckles pass him in on the air and rest on the water surface and his skin: some ash black, some more speckled white spots, but some are feathers.

Max lifts his hand from below the water. He sees the pigeon in the hands of the monster. The lifeless pigeon kicks no more on Max's palms. He has drowned the bird. No creature lives in this forest.

More speckles of white. Not feathers, not ash or char. These are tiny shreds of paper, which begin to confetti the water around him. A piece touches his face and sticks there in the wetness. Peeling it off, he examines it closely and sees words.

Quickly, Max splashes out of the water and runs, panicked, downstream. The pieces of paper he'd used to play the game are blowing away in the wind. Scattering everywhere, being whipped away. His stories are being lost to the wind.

Chapter 3

The Monster Inside

Grey liquid bubbles in a pot on top of the stove. Max watches, stirring. The liquid pops and plops, and a burning drop splashes his cheek. He pulls his face back from the steaming bucket. The soupy smell fills the room.

—

It is getting dark. And when the sun goes down here, the air turns icy cold. Winston tucks his face behind the collars of his shirt, but it does not stop the cold. As he reaches the carved stone at the foot of the mountain, he feels relief. He runs his fingers across the inscription on the flat rockface. He carved it on his very first night here, years ago. Mountains don't move, and this marker leads him home every day.

The lake shimmers below the forest floor in an arch-like horseshoe. Winston walks on until he sees it. The bunker hides from view, buried in the sloping dirt bank wall surrounding the lake. Winston and Max live right where the horse's little toe might be (if horses were to have toes). Burrowed into the dirty soil bank wall, under the roots of the forest floor, it is the smallest of the bunkers in the compound. As time has passed, needs have changed, and the dumps have furnished them with items of use.

—

'Hi, Grandad.'

Max greets Winston over his shoulder as he scrapes burnt soup from the walls of the pot. Max knows his hands are tell-tale cold from being outside. Grandad closes the door with a hard tug behind him. He tucks the rifle into the corner behind the door, clinking the empty whiskey bottles resting on the floor there. He slips out of the backpack straps. The artificial smell touches Winston's nose. He thinks about how he misses real food even more than rain while unpacking the bag onto the table.

'Hey, kiddo.'

Max stops, soup dripping from the spoon in his hand as he eyes the new thing Grandad has brought into the house. Grandad has never brought home anything like it before.

The boy dances indecisively with the dripping spoon before dropping it carelessly into the pot. He walks towards the thing Grandad has put behind the door.

'What's that?'

Winston empties the bag at his feet. The bottle is first, close to full with liquid. Then he pulls out new pages and the cloth wrap and leaves them on the table. While Max is distracted by the gun, he tucks the parcel onto his seat under the table.

'That's ... nothing, for now. I'll show you that later. I just want to sit for a minute.'

Maintenance bunkers are one large space. Max and Grandad have divided theirs with a curtain, so they have a two-room living space. On one side, away from the door, is the green curtain concealing two beds.

Their living quarters contain a kitchen consisting of wooden planks wedged into the corner, at an angle, supporting an aluminium basin. Nearby is a stove cobbled together from near-new parts and a wobbly table and three odd chairs. Winston has salvaged everything from the nearby dumps, each towering with near-new and brand-new items. People throw away the best of stuff, he always says, and there is no shortage of dumps around the edges of U City.

Winston takes his bottle and slumps into a tattered chair, filling the depression in its sunken, green cushioning. The high-back seat curves around his head whenever he sits back and raises his bottle to his lips. He doesn't choose to do this now. Instead, he sits forward, leaves the bottle by his feet and kicks off his mud-spattered boots onto the raggedy red rug.

He comforts in the soft wool under his stocking feet. It's rare his feet touch any surface that is not hard. He uses a large knitted doily to help part his feet from the dirt. Then he sits back for a moment, taking the daffodil from his breast pocket and twirling it idly between his fingers.

Winston feels a familiar draught around his head. He knows it's from the escape hole, a trap door opening in the forest floor above them, located high in the rear wall of this cavernous box. He feels comfort in this place. It smells human. The presence of people is a scent different from nature's flora and fauna. The smell is reassuring to him.

He looks up at the cactus roots, thick and wide, that have webbed across the ceiling. Over time, the roots have made their way through cracks and crevices in the metal. The cactus is dead now, but Winston still loves it. It is 'the only real tree in this forest.'

All trees look the same to Max. Real or fake. But Grandad says he can tell the difference.

'Watch how the wind swirls tighter to that tree than the others,' Grandad says. 'Even Mother Nature knows the difference.' But Max does not know who she is.

Grandad says he can see her, and even though he's always trying to point her out, Max can never see her. Whether they are inside, looking at the dirt floor or cactus roots, or standing at the door and looking out, Max has never been able to see this Mother Nature. This adds to Max's confusion.

'Soup's ready.' Max knows the soup is overcooked, having been left unsupervised all day. He wipes his hand on a cloth, still staring at the rifle in the corner. Winston sees the boy is distracted.

'It's … a … rifle.'

'What does it do?'

'It's a gun. Like the ones from some of our stories.'

'A gun?' Max's brow wrinkles in confusion. 'Where did you get it?'

'I've always had it, Max. I just keep it … outside the house.'

The old man rises from the chair, whiskey bottle and flower in hand.

'No more about the gun. I'm really hungry, and I bet you are too.'

Grandad places the whiskey on the table, feeling and hearing the empty movement in his stomach. He knows the boy's must feel the same.

'We don't have any C left,' said Max. 'This is just cactus needles.'

'None?'

Has it been worth it? Is all this worth it? Grandad wonders.

'Yes. We've been out of them since yesterday,' says Max, counting days backwards in his head while speaking.

'This will have to do us now, and I'll go to U City tomorrow.'

Grandad looks at the palms of his tired hands. They are filthy, holding the beautifully clean daffodil. Muck has dried beneath his fingernails and is smeared as high as his elbows. *Two days without C-protein.*

'I'll get a pack of C-cubes tomorrow. Promise. Do you want your birthday present?'

He places the flower on the new story pages and moves the parcel to the table. Max looks at it.

'Is it edible?'

'No, smart ass. Unfortunately not. I said I'll go tomorrow. I promise.' Winston hates visiting the U. Grandad steers Max to his chair by the shoulders. His is the one with its back to the door.

'Sit.'

Grandad looks into the pot on the stove. Max has let the spoon slide into the liquid. Taking two bowls from the shelf, he scoops each into the hot mess and brings them dripping to the table.

When his bowl touches the table, Max loses interest in his gift. He fills his mouth. Scoops his spoon. Fills his mouth. Scoops. Fills his mouth again.

It's only when the old man places his palms together and bows his head that Max stops, the spoon hovering an inch from his lips. The soup plops as he tips it slowly back into his bowl. Nothing makes a sound in this forest when it's windless. Max joins his hands and bows his head, but grace is silent. When Grandad raises his spoon, Max returns to filling his mouth.

Winston taps the parcel on the table.

'Happy birthday, kiddo.'

The old man tops off his soup with a shot from the whiskey bottle as Max's youthful hands go for the parcel. He unwraps two shoes. Max drops them to the floor, spinning on his seat to try them on.

'They're perfect. They don't match,' he said, pulling the yellow right shoe onto his foot.

'Yeah,' the old man confirms between spoonfuls.

Max pulls on the remaining pink shoe.

'It is hard enough to find two of the same shoe, but I start looking a while ago.'

What do you think? Max asks, posing newly shoed.

'That one's a little big. Loose but…'

'That's ok. I love them. Thank you, Grandad.'

'It is hard to find the same shoe or the same colour. Size would have taken even longer. They will do for now, and I'll keep checking the dumps.'

Max starts palming through the worn pages Grandad

has left on the table, looking at each one as if it is of sacred importance.

Winston takes another spoonful, sucking in cacti water before releasing the string on the cloth wrap on the table. A bundle of small wooden blocks roll out.

'What are those?'

'You remember that board I found a few months ago?'

Max nods, slurping the last of his soup.

'It's a game. These are the pieces. Just something I thought I could do at night after you've gone to bed. Keep my mind busy.'

Winston pours more whiskey into his soup bowl.

'Something productive. Have a look if you want.'

Max starts to remove the wooden pieces. He finds many uniquely shaped and others repeated – peeled, sliced, cut, etched and many stained. They must have taken hours of work. Max turns pieces in his hand, appreciating each individually.

'Soldiers?'

'Yeah. They're chess pieces. Here watch.'

Grandad brings the board to the table and stands the pieces in place. Meanwhile, Max pulls his journal from his waistband and slips the new story pages into the back, storing them safely within its covers. Then, taking Grandad's daffodil, he presses it between the centre pages of the journal beside the others. Thirteen years and thirteen daffodils.

Grandad's board is ready, each piece in its place. Max takes a pawn in his fingers.

'You wanna learn about this game?' says Grandad.

Max examines the little person-like head and wonders why the pawn has no eyes.

'Your mam loved it. It's a great game,'

Winston eyes his mother's journal on the table.

'Often cruel, this game. And complex.'

Max admires the whittling in his hand. Seeing Max's watchful eye distracted, Winston picks up the bottle of whiskey and walks to the pot of soup.

'It's a game that requests player skills.'

He turns his back to the boy and busies himself at the stove. Max turns the dirty new pages from his mother, stopping to read brief snatches. He knows the bottle is in Grandad's hands, hidden from view.

Winston spoons a brown powder into a chipped enamel cup. The cup, once white, is now stained brown too.

'It's a game of black versus white, man versus woman, one player against another.'

Winston adds whiskey and turns to place the cup on the table.

'A game designed to divide.'

Winston reads the green lettering APZON on the coffee label. He grimaces and turns the bag, facing the label against the wall. Max's nose wrinkles as the coffee steam reaches his nostrils. Recalling the stink by the lake earlier today, he realises coffee is no longer the worst smell in the world. Grandad sits down to face Max and, in one swig, empties the cup. He reaches across and flips the pages of Max's journal, jabbing the first page with a dirty finger. He knows the words will distract the boy, and he refills the cup with the whiskey bottle tucked beneath his elbow.

'I'll teach you this game,' Grandad says, emptying his cup again, 'between the chapters.' Grandad doesn't like Max's habit of reading only the beginnings of stories. Max wants to read about exciting new worlds that are not like his own, but he prefers to stop before the second act. He doesn't like where the protagonist is forced to change and where trouble interjects into their world. At this point, Max always wants to stop reading and begin another story. He prefers to retain his feeling of hope in a brand new world and avoid the inevitable struggle. Winston points at the open book again.

'This was your Mam's favourite story when she was thirteen. I remember giving it to her when she was little, even younger than you are now, and she loved it instantly, carried it with her everywhere, asked questions constantly.'

Winston chuckles at the memory.

'She was a small girl asking questions about souls, and who does or doesn't have one, life, death, all these big questions.'

He smiles with glazed eyes.

'It drove people crazy.' He remembers those family gatherings when the adults tried to avoid her. Grandad slumps back, cherishing fond memories.

Max rolls one of the pawns between his fingers and palm and smiles in pleasure at his grandad's whittle work.

'Thank you, Grandad,' he says as he repositions the pawn into its place on the chessboard and raises the white king again in admiration.

'You're welcome, kiddo. Or should I say, young man?'

Grandad feels his eyes blur with sudden tears. 'Now, do you want to start reading and I'll take chapter two?'

He swigs back the end of a cupful of coffee. Then he lowers the cup back to the table, removes the bullets from his pocket and drops them in it. The metal is makeshift ice, chilled from being outside in the night air. He tops the cup up with whiskey.

Max clears his throat and reads the title of his mother's favourite story.

'Frankenstein: a modern Prometheus.'

—

The soup is cold. Grandad's eyes closed three chapters ago, and Max has read alone.

He sees Winston's eyes open momentarily to look into his empty whiskey cup. And then they shut again.

Max looks over his shoulder to the corner. The rifle is close. Grandad's snores cause the pages of the journal to gently flap as Max reaches for the handle of the gun. It's heavier than he expects. At first, it feels awkward, but then he finds a comfortable way to hold it. His palm folds around the smooth handle. They fit.

Wondering how it will feel to aim the gun, he raises it and pushes the rest into his shoulder. He waves it a bit. It's not that heavy. And suddenly, his thoughts are interrupted as a single grey pigeon feather floats before him, sinking in the centre of the room. Max raises the sight to his eye and finds this feather at the opposite end. He slips his finger through the trigger ring as he hears his grandad grunt and sees his grandfather's eyes open in the sight. He holds the rifle on the old man as the feather sails to the floor. Max feels the trigger and thinks about Monsters and Frankensteins and doctors and souls and mothers and grandfathers.

Winston is instantly sober as he wakes to the sight of a rifle barrel aimed at him. He is awake. He is sure of it. And that look is back in the boy's eye. He has seen it once before though many years have passed since. Winston rises slowly. Max remains perfectly still, the rifle sight fixed now on his grandad's gut. Winston steps closer, unsure whether the boy is even breathing he is so still. He barely dares to breathe himself as he gently takes the rifle by the barrel and lifts it from Max's hand. Relieved, he wraps an arm around the young boy's shoulders, ushering him towards his bed.

'Come on; all these stories appear too much for your imagination.'

Grandad tucks Max in under his blankets.

'Sleeping should be done in bed. Not up and about.'

He pulls the blanket under Max's chin, and Winston breathes freely again only when the boy's eyes close. That look is gone. The old man returns to the table and slugs the last of the whiskey from the bottle.

He reaches into his breast pocket as he lifts the gun. He finds the gun is stiff to open but sees it remains reasonably rust-free. There is a bullet now in the chamber. One bullet for the boy, one for Winston himself and one spare. Had this bullet been the one intended for Winston?

Winston thinks of Max. *Is it worth it? Is all this going to be worth the effort? How important is keeping a promise?*

Or was this the bullet intended for Max? Grandad points

the loaded rifle at his sleeping grandson. Winston can end it all now in two bullets. *And the spare would go unused.*

—

Lumpy, our camel friend, survives all this time. The red 'X' sprayed on his side, marking him for slaughter, is almost gone now. The sun has faded it, and time has flaked it off. Thirteen years have passed since he emerged through the hole in the wall.

Lumpy has stuck mainly to the trees. The trees offer some shade from the sun though the heat remains. Camels are good with heat. He sees the tarmac road, but he avoids it. The road leads straight into U City. Lumpy stays away as there's nothing for him there.

—

Winston folds Max's clothes into a neat square and stacks them on the foot of the bed. It's in the right pants pocket that he finds another of the bullets that was taken from the cup while Grandad slept. Watching Max closely, Grandad returns the bullet to the breast pocket of his shirt. Even two might now prove to be more troublesome than Grandad ever foresaw. Three were too many. That bullet would remain out of the game until a time when it might be needed.

Chapter 4

Learning to Shoot

Morning comes with a headache. Stiff, Winston peels himself from the kitchen table and stumbles like a newborn deer. A full fresh pot of water boils on the stove, and he feels his stomach rumbling. Max is reading, his belly on the rug. The boy is a soothing sight to Winston's burning eyes. Winston sips his coffee before he balls up the empty APZON coffee package in his fist. The sound in the silent morning pulls Max back out from the page.

'Morning, Grandad.'

'Morning, kiddo.'

Max kicks his legs behind him with no headache.

'I have to go to the post-box today,' says Winston, standing the empty whiskey bottle in the sink. He remembers last night's events, or at least, he tries to remember.

I deserved one, Winston thinks. *I'm so close to having the right mix now. I have dug a further foot ... plus it was a birthday party. I was allowed one drink. One's no harm. Thirteen years, one whiskey, commemorate.*

The shocking headache interrupts his thread of thought,

and his fingers rise to sooth his throbbing brow. Another sip of coffee. *That's the last of the coffee,* he reminds himself.

He knows he must go, but he hates going to U City. He stares into the empty cup for a moment and then, with a start, realises that the weapon is no longer on the table.

'Max? Where is the rifle?'

'It's in my room.'

'Why is it in your room?'

'I've been looking at it.'

Grandad has many questions, but Max's eyes do not leave the pages. He is rereading from the journal.

Grandad slips into the sleeping side of the curtain and returns holding the rifle.

'You are curious about this?'

Max looks up from the floor.

'I just wanted to see how it worked and ...'

'These things, and all the others like them cause nothing but pain. Weapons are designed to cause death. Nobody should take life away. Damn the man who made a tool for doing so.'

Winston's stomach rumbles. Max closes the book and clambers up from the floor, Winston opens the gun at the hinge. He finds only one bullet in the chamber.

How many had he loaded into it? Did he shoot it last night while drunk? Did Max? He struggles to remember, and his head hurts more as he tries.

The city can wait till later. Regardless of how hungry they both are, Max needs to learn to respect the new item.

'Go get dressed.'

Max follows his grandad's instruction, watching the old man as he does.

'Something you can wear outside.'

—

The old man takes four empty bottles from behind the door and gathers the rifle. Max offers to take the gun. But Grandad loads the bottles into his backpack and tells Max to get the door.

On the table sits last night's game board. Checkmate white. The game had ended long before the book had. And long before he had fallen asleep. Winston struggles to recall the events exactly. Max was white. How does a small boy beat an experienced chess player at chess, having never played the game before?

Winston finds himself swearing off whiskey once again.

'Stay close to me. Do as I ask, and this will be fine,' he says. 'Stay near.'

Winston ducks out the entrance. Max doesn't hesitate and follows him out.

—

'You see this rock?'

Max's head nods.

'Pay attention. It's not just a rock. It's this rock.'

Winston drags four fingers across a line on the rock.

A letter with a series of numbers is etched in the rock above a message: *M7:26*

And every one that heareth these words of mine, and doeth them not, shall be likened unto a foolish man, which built his house upon the sand.

'This rock is home. It's at this rock we start, and when we see this rock, we know we are home,' Winston explains.

The woods are narrow but long. All colours of brown, they curve at the foot of the mountain range, and around the lake.

They walk for hours through the trees, water on their right and the mountain slope on their left. They see the city in the distance as the morning passes. For the first time, Max sees the lights of U City. They are bright enough and in such multitude that they are visible by day. And constant. At this distance in the forest, the glow of Utopia city is visible. The Citadel at the centre, is brightest of all.

Max sees the green-coned beacon of the Citadel. APZON's main building is levels higher than any of the other buildings of the Central City.

'What's that Grandad?'

'That's nothing,' the old man replies. 'What did I say? Keep your eyes on where you're going.'

Winston is on high alert.

'We're sticking to this side of the water. Now pay attention. You need to remember this way, Max.'

They hear the crunch of undergrowth beneath their feet as they move through the trees. A fine sand blows in the air. Max can feel it on his skin. He scratches the back of his hand where the pigeon pecked him.

Grandad marches on, sobering up. Meanwhile, Max skips along or stops when he's distracted by the itching of his pecked hand. At times, he has to run to catch up with the old man.

'What are you scratching at all the time? Stop scratching,' says Winston, stopping in the silence of the forest. He kneels, unpacks his backpack on the forest floor, and slings the rifle strap around himself as he gets to his feet.

'Ok, you see this?'

Winston points at a large metal box in the forest.

'What is it?'

'This is a pump, Max.'

Grandad points into the woods.

'The next pump is right there. You can see it,'

'What does it do?'

'It pumps water. Listen!'

Winston points again.

'Go line those bottles up on top of the far pump. And then come straight back here, you understand?'

Max looks at the empty whiskey bottles.

'Pay attention to your footing.'

Winston's tone is firm.

'Be as fast as you can. Do not wander, and do not touch anything.'

Max scurries across the divide between the two pumps. The bottles in his arms clink, pressed against his chest.

Reaching the pump, he rests the bottles. He tries to see inside through a pump vent. He wonders if there is a better view from the other side. The vent door on top is already lifted on one side. Up on his toes, he manages to push it open although not wide enough to fit his entire head. His face darkens in the shadow of the small vent door, and he recognises the smell inside from the lake.

Fascinated, Max stares down into the pit beneath the pump housing, easily 20 feet deep. The journal, shoved in his waistband, pushes against his stomach as he leans in to see better. Thousands of run-off pipes flower out beneath the soil. They rise up to the sprinklers on top of the pump, and cloudy, rotten-smelling water pumps through sprinklers onto the trees.

The snap of a nearby twig makes him pull his head from inside the pump-housing. He glances around, picturing the return of the hulking Monster-man from the lake. Max realises that he saw Frankenstein hours before reading the story. Before Grandad and he read the story, there was a memory, a trace of the Monster in his head.

He finds no cause for the noise and sees nothing but trees. However with his awareness heightened, he listens and watches for movement in the trees. Max has learnt to live in a forest, and learnt to ignore the forest's constant sounds. He no longer hears the creaking of tall trees as they sway at their tips.

He hears that creaking now, and his eyes rise to the tree tops. The rays of the setting sun reach in through the thickness of the forest, shooting down in beams between the leaves. The trees sway open, then closed, open and closed, open and closed. Swaying trees. The wind seems stronger up there. The light appears and disappears between the trees as if nature is parting to let Max's eye see what happens in the sky next.

Max closes his eyes with the sun on his face. The swaying trees close, then nothing. No sunlight. The shadow stays on

Max's face. Though the wind and creaking sound remains, his face is in shadow. Instead of light, there is sound.

Sssshhhh ...

The sound comes from above the treetops. It sounds like a draught, or an intense wind. Max looks up and sees nothing but trees. He stands looking up, watching in the shadows. Waiting for the trees to part so he can see this *sssshhhhing* shade-caster.

The noise moves across the sky, above the leaves again. Out of sight. Concealed by the tree leaves. And then he hears another sound overhead in the sky.

Sccchu ...

A sound like air swiping. Max knows of nothing that can be lighter than air. Nothing can fly in the sky over his head. His eyes have never anything fly. The grey living thing by the lake. Could it have come down from the sky too? Is it possible for something to walk through the air as Max does on the ground?

The tree tops part and gently spread and Max watches a large triangular-shaped object pass over. It slides through the sky, over the forest, briefly blotting out the light from the low sun. And he could swear he sees the outline of a person on this triangle.

He hears another snap, something breaking underfoot, this one closer to him. A hand reaches out from between the leaves, parting them like a curtain. Grandad steps out from between the forestry, panting slightly. Max looks back up for the flying thing. He hopes to see it again, maybe more clearly this time. He is ready.

But the sky is empty and getting darker. There is no sound.

'What did I say?' says Winston frowning.

'Sorry, Grandad.'

Max is happy to see him and follow as Winston returns to the first pump.

Grandad places the rifle on top of the pump housing, and pulling himself up on top, crawls on his stomach across the old water pump.

Max follows and sits where the old man pats his hand. With one hand, Winston touches his forehead, then below the chest, his left side and then his right. Max thinks he's making a sign like a cross on his body. Grandad rolls flat on his belly and pushes his face up against butt of the rifle.

Max does not blink. He's so still that he can feel his heart rate slow down. He watches Grandad's hands.

'We have to learn precision. Our target will always be small. We always only ever aim for hands, legs, feet.'

Winston speaks commandingly.

'No man has the right to take another life. You remember the story? It is a sin to kill a mockingbird. Does Doctor Frankenstein have the right to end the monster's life just because he created it? No. Calling it a monster might soothe his conscience – but it's a sin, still.

'To responsibly stop a target without taking their life requires a lot of knowledge and practice. That will start today. You are old enough now. And I am getting older.'

Max looks down the length of the rifle in Grandad's hands. He looks straight at Grandad again. Then at the gun.

Then Grandad as he speaks again.

'They can take lives. So we have to know how to survive, with responsibility.'

Max is bewildered.

'What will we have to shoot? This forest is empty?'

Winston thinks in silence for a moment.

'Yes.'

The older man manoeuvres himself.

'Get in here behind it the gun.'

Max shuffles over and tucks himself in behind the rifle.

'Ok, you see this? You look through here as I did. Lift this when you want to see.'

The old man moves the boy like a puppet as he speaks.

'Shoulder here, cheek here, hand, legs, toes, elbows, just like you saw Grandad do it.'

Winston looks out into the trees through binoculars.

'Can you see the other pump?'

Winston pans the binoculars. The empty bottles are standing on the top of the next pump just as Max left them.

'You see the bottles?'

Winston eyes each of the bottles. He can only see one at a time through the view finder.

'Ok, we only have ... one bullet. So make the best of the single shot. When you are ready, I want you to ...'

Grandad is startled as gunshot breaks the air. The old man scans the bottles again. The first is gone. So is the second. They're all gone. Grandad cannot see any of them. He lowers the binoculars and squints into the distance.

'What happened?'

Grandad looks across his shoulder at the little boy.

'Did you hit them?'

Max is still, silent and concentrating. He is not breathing and doesn't answer. Winston lifts the peak of his cap and climbs off the pump's metal housing.

'I'm just gonna ... go see ... pick up any glass. Don't want anyone finding ...'

But Max is no longer paying attention. The gun is empty so he has lost interest in it. He removes the journal from his waistband and begins to read. His endless potential is lost to him in his innocence and naivety.

'I'll be back in a second,' the old man says. 'Don't move. This is a very dangerous forest.'

Winston leaves the empty rifle on top of the pump, but the boy is only interested in his journal now. He slides off the pump with the open journal in his hand, sitting on the ground cross-legged to read.

Winston leaves him to it. He knows he can be across to the next pump and back in a few minutes if he hurries. He wants to see what exactly has happened to the bottles. And he cannot leave broken glass to be found.

He sees Max has cleared the row of bottles, smashing them all with one bullet. The boy instinctively knew the precise point to hit that first bottle so that it exploded with enough force to shatter the surrounding ones. Winston wonders at the boy's precision and steady hand to make the shot without practice or experience.

In Max's world, the forest is gone for the moment: no cold wind with bristly feel of sand; no hard ground beneath his bottom; no fluttering leaves or creaking tall trees. He is in his story, in a laneway in 17th century Geneva where a monster of a man sits curled up and crouched.

From whom would such a powerful and large man have to hide? No one could be a physical threat to a man of this size. No one man indeed, but a village full could. The scared man hides, cowering as the villagers pass the entrance to the wet and dark laneway.

He stays silent, so they do not hear him, fearing they will tear him apart. Max reads intently. Until a stick beneath his elbow cracks, and the snap echoes through the silent forest.

The sound reaches the laneway in Geneva above the clamour of the fire-breathing crowd. The monster uncovers his hiding face at the sound of the snap as if he heard Max. There's another sound, and Max looks into the trees to see the face of a young girl looking back at him. She is feet away from where he sits. He can see her through the leaves, and she can see him.

He does not recognise her nor remember any story from which she might have fallen. She's older than Max by a year or two, maybe. Which it is, does not matter. She is too young to be out in the forest alone. Max knows that. And where has she come from? Max has never seen another person in the forest. Max has never seen another person other than Grandad. However, here she is alone. He realises he too is alone. They are both alone – and together.

Her hair is brown and matted together in thick, snake-like locks that get thinner in width and lighter in colour until the brown is blonde at their ends. She has something in her hand. Is it…? Panicked, Max glances around the forest floor. His journal is gone. The bushes rustle, and the girl is gone. Running. Through those trees and away from him – with his book.

Instinctively, Max slaps the stump of the rifle, sending it corkscrewing in the air. He catches it, his left hand searching in his pocket.

Where is it? The bullet. He remembers taking it from the cup and putting it in his pocket. Where can it have gone?

It doesn't matter, it's not there. He's off, running after her to retrieve that book.

She jumps rocks, ducks branches and leaps over half-fallen trees. Max struggles at first, but quickly learns the skipping, hopping, climbing and ducking that running through a forest demands.

He gains on her. He has her almost in his reach and stretches out a hand for her shoulder. Suddenly, a large mass of something hits him hard from the side, knocking him off his feet.

'What the hell are you doing?' the mass yells.

A long black rectangular bar runs up each side of the tree next to his head on the forest floor. Max realises he was inches from passing the laser line.

'Those things would have cut your head off!' says Grandad, kissing Max's head between his large rough palms. 'What were you thinking, you idiot boy?'

The old man pulls Max back tight to his chest, holding him for a time in silence.

Max hears the sound of something snapping in the forest

floor again. He questions whether the sound comes from the world or his imagination, but realises it comes from beyond the laser line on the other side of the forest.

Winston heard the noise too. He loosens his grip on Max and steps closer to invisible line they dare not cross.

'Did you see something, Max? Why were you running?'

The old man holds Max back from the laser's sensor with a hand on the boy's shoulder. He leans his own face inches from the laser line.

'Did you see anything?'

Grandad turns and grips the boy by both shoulders and kneels on a single knee before him.

'Do you see anything in these trees?'

Max runs his eyes across the forest behind Grandad.

'Max, did you see something?'

The girl looks out from behind a tree trunk and looks into Max's eyes.

From beyond the line, twelve trees in and four trees over, she watches him. She does not look away when she sees him see her.

'No,' says Max, staring into the green of this mysterious girl's eyes.

'No Grandad. I didn't see anything. I just ...'.

'Just..?'

The old man tries to coax the words out quicker.

'I just got turned around and didn't know where I was ... sorry, Grandad.'

Winston pulls Max to his chest again and holds him there for several moments. The wind parts the trees above, and the darkening sky above reminds Winston it's getting late.

Winston walks slower on the way home. His eyes are constantly on their surroundings, watching the forest.

Max thinks about his journal. Now it's gone. She took it. He regrets bringing it at all. He replays the events in his mind. The only physical memory he has of his mother were those transcribed words, and he has lost them.

Who is that girl? Can I ever find her again? Get the book back? I lost the book and my bullet.

By the time the moon has curled fully around overhead and night has arrived, Max and Grandad have hung their coats on hooks inside the bunker door. The sandy residue from the wind now dusts the floor.

Moonlight juts down through rusted holes in the bunker walls and ceiling. The light slices very precisely, across the floor of the room. In the flick of a switch, the moonlight is gone. Thankfully the electricity has never been cut off from the bunkers. They are still in the compound grid, and the entire compound powers itself.

Soon the last of their water is boiling in a small pot on the stove. Empty bottles wait by the door for refilling when Grandad finally goes into the city.

Grandad watches Max lying on the floor in the corner. The boy's little eyes are fixed with a concentration that Winston envies. He has not been able to achieve such focus since arriving here. He finds his mind is constantly hopping, but Max is in what he calls 'flow' while playing a chess match against himself. As the water bubbles, Winston stares at the young boy and longs for that ability again.

The old man sees himself inches from youth. If only he could walk across the room and through time back towards himself at that age. Here is age and youth just feet apart in a small space that's split with an impassable line. No one can walk back years.

Winston sits at the table and starts cleaning the gun. Having ragged it down in oil, he points the rifle at the small boy. Trains the sight on his grandson. Then he waits, expecting tears to come to his eyes. Winston has not cried in what he estimates must be decades. He tries to remember.

He definitely cried in his teenage years. He might have cried during the decades he called his twenties and thirties. However, he knows for certain he has not cried since then. He is 65 now. That is maybe 35 years since he has seen tears from the inside out. He wonders is that a skill he has lost? Or is it an ability he has gained? Thirty-five years, no tears. And there are no tears now.

He keeps the gun trained on Max. His hand stays as steady as the very mountain on top of their house; steady-handed as if a younger man with a younger hands holds the gun.

As the old man pushes down the hammer, he tries to drag up a feeling from within himself. Something, anything will do. A feeling of any sort, something that might affect his gut rather than his head for once. Some emotion that will stop him shooting Max now and ending it. Something to prove he can still feel.

Winston closes his eyes and hears the wind blow outside. Then the warm air pops. Dry lightning flashes the room in brightness and lights up everything in the room, even the inside of Winston's head behind his closed eyes.

As the wind chases itself on the other side of the door, it rattles the door in its frame. Winston takes a slow breath and decides.

Chapter 5

Into the Utopian City

For a few minutes after waking, Winston keeps his eyes shut. He stretches. He then opens his eyes before swinging his legs off the cushioned shelf he calls his bed. Hobbling with stiff bones, he passes Max's bed. It is unprecedented for Max not to be in his bed. But he looks, and Max is not in it.

Once dressed, Winston kneels by the rug. He lifts it and takes the flat card-key underneath. Fixing the rug back down, he makes sure it's straight. Soon, he's quietly and quickly moving through the forest far beyond the engraved rock.

Travelling light with a single pack on his back, he is quick-footed for an old man. Winston knows he once did this trip in half the time. However, he accepts, he was younger then. It used to be easier back then. However, it was more stressful as he often chose to leave the infant child sleeping.

The sack on his back is full and bounces behind his shoulders. He fished the plastic out of the water over the course of four weeks, the usual space between his trips into U City. He reaches his first destination. Peeling back a leafy net, he reveals the car: the Pawn. Winston stares at its chrome grill, grinning back at him almost mockingly.

Is it smirking at me? he thinks. *Or just smirking in general?* It smirks even when covered and hiding, constantly thinking it's superior. *Only a prick like Adam Skinner could make such a vehicle,* thinks Winston. *I knew that boy had a superiority complex from the moment my daughter brought him home.*

He tries to shake off the memories of Skinner. *Perhaps the car is just smiling because it's being taken back in the road.* No matter how much he hates the sight of the old electric car, he still needs it every now and then. He gets in, shuts the door and the plastic card-key finds its slot in the dash. Winston prays it starts.

The Pawn, a Model 1 is another APZON production – and the first electric vehicle of its type. The model 1 is outdated now. They have reached the Model 6. However, the newest one is almost identical. As are all the ones between. All that has changed is the name and a few variations in the shape. The streets of the U are flooded with APZON cars – some Model 5s but mostly Model 6s since their release last week. Grandad's car will stand out like a fossil. But the tech inside has not changed. There is no reason why the Model 1 will not continue to work. It should work as long as they do not change the roads, and Winston knows they have not. But Winston still prays it starts.

It starts.

He knew it would.

Winston still cannot bring himself to look into the back seat. He knows the seat remains blood stained. Blood can be washed from fabric though it requires a lot of work. Blood cannot be washed off the mind. Somethings cannot be washed away. He has never had the stomach to try. He is momentarily lost in thought. Behind his eyes, he sees Max's face, as the boy is now – age 13 and remembers his first sight of the boy.

Up until then, he was sure he'd never hold a grandson. Sarah never even wanted children, and Winston had been OK with that. Winston never believed he'd hold his baby's baby. He certainly never believed he'd hold his grandson while the mother bled to death.

Which to help first? She, his own child or Max, so small and helpless. The baby's face matures in Grandad's mind. Then blood fiercely splatters across Winston's memory. Max's birth day. Winston wipes the images from his thoughts, and he heads for U City.

Part of him wishes the engine hasn't started. He wishes so every time. No matter how long he has left it neglected, no matter how old it gets, it still starts and runs without fuelling. *The bastarding thing never gives up.*

The Bastarding Pawn. That's what Skinner should call these models, Winston thinks as the vehicle's emblem swings on chain from the mirror.

—

In darkness of the bunker, Max covers his pillow with a blanket. It looks as he intends – his size and shape. It looks as if he is still curled up and asleep. *Hopefully.* In the kitchen the chessboard remains on the table from the night before. Max sneaks across trying not to wake the old man. He stops to look at the board unable to pass it.

He sees the pieces for the first time in daylight. Grandad has fashioned the pieces from trees older than himself. He has whittled unique cuts and nicks into each one. Each cut and edge intended to make the piece identifiable: a queen that is worth more than a bishop, a bishop more than a pawn. And Grandad has blackened half the set with a flame.

The board sits there in its endgame position, waiting to be reset. The king remains trapped. A king is never taken. Never defeated. Just the knowledge that he is defeated ends the game. And it begins all over again. The king always lives on to fight again.

Max shuts his eyes. He can still see the board, the pieces and their positions in his mind. And behind his closed eyes, he knows he can rewind the entire game – 321 moves – from memory. An inhuman-like feat. Move after move, he remembers each one and the correct order. Backwards. He brings the two sides to their original line formations. An exact rewind of the match.

At the door of the bunker, Max stands in silence and feels the night's breeze. Looking back at the curtain between himself and the sleeping old man, Max reconsiders. He could stop now and no harm is done. Staring out into the forest, he waits for a decision. For just a moment, a road of chequered tiles leads to the doorway. Each brick has a word written within it.

Max steps out onto the bricks and the words. He recognises them as the words he has read hundreds of times. The words his mother lived by and which his grandad transcribed and brought back to him. And the words that he has lost.

As he walks further away from the bunker he realises, he had not lost them. The book may be gone, stolen by some mysterious girl, but here they are again. The words are still in him. He reads them now again as he walks and moves far from home.

—

The emblem dangling from the rear view mirror is a small wooden pawn wrapped in a silver ring. It clinks against the window as the car moves. The smell inside the car is a blend of things. To Winston it smells like death – and life.

Winston leaves the mountain behind as he crosses the bridge into the city. He rolls in under the shadow of the towering city and the bright lights of U City's sky-scraping metropolis.

U City is an urban Utopia dreamed by an eccentric billionaire. It runs logistically perfect, created like nothing else created before. One man's dream on a blank canvas.

The pawn swings and clinks against the window screen as Winston glances up at the building tops. A voice within the cab tells Winston of the current weather and forecasts. The battery indicator-light climbs to green telling the driver that the vehicle has fully self-charged.

Winston smiles unable to help himself. He look around, impressed by the majesty of the city despite himself.

'It works. It all works,' says Winston aloud him with a slight feeling of pride.

The Pawn looks more comfortable now that it is out of the trees, among curves and lights more similar to its own. Admittedly, it's older than all the other vehicles, but it is part of this Utopian compound.

The windows open and circulate the smell of blood from deep within the cushioning of the back seat. Only someone who knows it is there will smell it. Winston can still smell the blood. Soon, he's driving deep in the city and sees people everywhere. Coming and going – swarming as they start their day. They are moving in all directions: scooting, walking, running. And lines and lines of people queue outside store fronts. They line up, their necks arched back to read the scrolling billboards above. Above the store front doors, above the traffic signals, on every building side and bus stop are digital billboards, constantly rolling messages – sales pitches. One advertisement, appearing more regularly than others, displays a timer that's counting down

65 hours, 40 minutes, 20 seconds to the release of The Key Model 12 ...

It's the latest APZON handheld device.

The Pawn stops without making a sound. Winston steps out of the Pawn into the parking lot under the skyscrapers. Now morning has arrived and lights are extinguished, the buildings are less impressive. Things can hide in shadows. Winston turns to face the Bodega plastic-exchange store. The mountains he lives beneath are over his shoulder, waiting for his return.

U City is purpose-designed. A four-lane motorway like an artery runs perpendicular from the centre of the city to the foot of the mountain. When the sun sets behind the mountain, the town fills with darkness like the sand filling an egg-timer.

Smaller roads lead off the four-lane motorway. They splinter like a spiderweb or like arteries pumping blood to every point of the city, allowing access to this pinnacle of the economy. U City is the home of retail, data-storage, employment and living space with the Citadel at its core.

Grandad stands in the carpark on the retail side of Main Street. The Citadel looms large, tall enough to be visible from anywhere within the compound. Winston knows it can be seen even within parts of the forest and for him, feels like an oppressive force. He knows what's contained within it.

The Citadel, a towering green pin from within the trees, is useful for navigation. Here, embedded in the impressiveness of the city, it is mesmerising: a cone of dazzling glass, light and steel. Such is its great height, that every eye is drawn to it. It inspires everyone in the city to embody the message the company represents. And it has the power to corrupt even Winston who knows its truth.

The old man shakes himself out of his reverie and throws the Citadel a sneering glance. He checks if anybody nearby is watching and then goes about what he came to do.

He opens the rear passenger door of the Pawn, and any feelings of determination vanish when Max looks up at him from the rear footwell of the car. He has been lying across the floor and behind the fronts seats all along.

A time of silence passes between them, and Winston uses it to think what to do next.

'I had to come, Grandad.'

Winston looks across the car park at the plastic-exchange. He has parked, as always, at the far side of the carpark. Now he is relieved about his cautious habit. The plastic-exchange store has large windows that overlook the car park, but its occupants can't see the boy from where Grandad has parked.

Winston thinks.

It may look suspicious if he gets back in the truck and disappears. Also, if he doesn't exchange the plastic, they will not eat. They have not eaten a proper meal with protein cubes in two days. They are both hungry.

He can take Max home and return to the exchange but having the Pawn 1 on the road for so long risks attracting attention. Best to be on the road as little as possible.

Max interrupts Winston's racing thoughts.

'I just want to see what it is like.'

Offensive plays often require a sacrifice.

The old man lifts the sack of salvaged plastic out of the back of the e-car.

'Look. But do not get out of that car. Do you hear me? ...'

Winston doubts his decision for just a second but continues.

'Do not be seen, and don't draw attention to either of us.'

Grandad removes the key from the slip in the dash, and the roof glass blackens. Max can no longer see the sky through it. The old man walks casually towards the exchange.

Max doesn't move. As instructed, he remains there, lying on his back until he can't resist it anymore. He refuses to miss the opportunity of seeing the outside world after coming this far. Lifting himself, he stretches his neck and peeks out the window. He sees the Citadel and his eyes rake the structure from its peak in the sky to its steel and glass base. He has never seen or known anything like it. He follows this majesty of the building with his eyes. The only tall structures Max knows are trees, and this, the Citadel, is no tree.

His eyes meet the activity of the road, and he's distracted by that. His eyes run along a cityscape that is full of people, towering buildings, things moving here and there, fast and slow. Things Max does not understand. Twisting and turning in the car, Max sees more and more. He follows the road back in the other direction away from the Citadel and towards the mountain slopes. Home.

He looks back to the retail area and the plastic-exchange. He's no longer peeking. His face is pressed in awe to the window, and he realises he's in full view of any onlookers. He doesn't care. He's willing to risk it for a better look.

A loud noise, metal clashing against metal, startles him. The feeling of bravery is gone, and he drops back down out of view into the footwell. He can still hear it. Now they are knocking sounds. He keeps his head down but not for long. Max dares a peek. He can see Grandad's back on the opposite side of the parking lot, entering the exchange.

The noises come from the side of a nearby store. A girl is crawling out from under the tilted lid of a bulky metal box. He watches her close the lid of the large metal bin. She moves like a fox. Staying low around the waste box, she dips her head below the store window as she circles around to the front door. And she goes in.

Her knotted snakes of hair seem longer, and she looks taller, but he knows her. She is the girl from the forest. The girl who took his book.

—

A group of youths loiter at the door of the exchange as Winston approaches. *I can only control the moves I make,* he thinks. The next seconds will require his restraint, especially now Max is present. The old man makes his way through the group crowding the entrance, but brushes against one of the adolescents. The boy raises his eyes from a device in his hand, and watches Grandad enter the store.

—

Max watches as his grandad goes inside. Max considers and makes the decision. He opens the rear door of the Pawn and eases himself out through the smallest space between the car door and body. It surprises even him to find himself standing outside on a surface his feet have never touched before.

He closes the e-car door. Through the window, he notices for the first time the blood stained seats. A birthmark on the rear seat of the Pawn.

Max stands erect and confidently walks across the carpark. He's so casual that not a single head turns. He looks as if he's always done this. Max enters the store just as he watched the girl do. He decides it best to copy the other's mannerisms and not draw any attention to himself. A light tinkling of a bell sounds from above Max's head as he steps over the threshold. Almost instantly, a foraging noise inside the store stops abruptly as if he's disturbed someone. The forest girl springs up from behind a counter and stares at Max.

'Hello,' she says, 'how can I help you today?'

'You work here?'

The forest girl nods her head.

Max looks around. APZON Grocery Stores stock a great many fascinating items. Before he realises, he is scanning two lines of shelving intrigued by items he's never seen before.

He reads labels: 'healthy', 'energy', 'low-fat', 'sugar-free' and 'eco-friendly' branded on crisps and cakes, dips and bars, sweets and gum. They all look inviting, but he cannot linger and approaches the counter.

'You took my book!'

'What? I'm kinda busy. Working.'

The girl says this with a nervous jitter.

'In the middle of something. You want a book or something ...?'

A noise emerges from what appears to be the stockroom behind the girl, and she jumps.

'Look, kid, you want something from the store? I'm in hurry.'

Max thinks.

'Water. My grandad and I came for water. To refill our bottles and sell our plastic.'

But he's distracted again – this time by the girl's clothing. The girl is wearing a black t-shirt with the Prince album cover, Purple Rain, adorning the front. A large red X has been spray painted across the image.

'What is Purple Rain?'

'Purple Rain? It's an old record from this artist Prince. My dad told me. Prince is pretty awesome.'

'So why the X? If he's so awesome?'

'Oh it's a statement against the Purple Rain software. I made it myself. What do you think?'

'Purple Rain software?'

Max has no idea what she's referring to.

'Purple Rain? The software that superseded Deep Blue.'

Max is still bewildered.

'What world are you from weird kid?' she exclaims.

'Max. My name is Max. Not wierdkit. And I'm from this world. At least I think so.'

'I'm Alex,' says the girl, 'and Deep Blue was the first software to ever beat a human being at chess. Purple Rain superseded Deep Blue and is now currently the greatest software program capable of playing the game. And some suggest actually being capable of thinking for itself. Really problematic shit. And something we strongly fight against.'

'We?' he adds.

The girl's brow furrows into a V-shape.

'Yeah, we. My family and all the other families are fighting. Listen kid, I don't know what's up with you, but everybody in this city is slowly seeing their humanity erased. We are being manipulated by APZON products.

'Our whole community are trying to bring APZON down and give people a chance to think for themselves again. People used to think for themselves once. Did you know that? At least that's what my dad says. And the other elders too.'

The stockroom door swings open with a draft, and more noise emerges. Alex glances at it and begins to hurry. She connects a small cable into her phone and the other end into the back of the cash point.

'Look, kid, you're staring at me and the candy since you walked in. You can't buy me so here…'

She grabs some chocolate from the shelf behind her.

'Have yourself some candy bars.'

She eyes a stack of brown bags. Peeling one from the top, she shoves it full of the chocolate bars and rolls the bag closed.

'On the house. Get out.'

She pushes the bag against Max's chest and starts disconnecting her phone from the cash point.

Max suddenly realises she doesn't work in the store. In fact, Alex is taking from the store just as she took his book. Max wants to ask about the book, but he hears a noise from the stockroom. Someone is approaching.

'In the forest, my book … that was you, wasn't it?'

Max knows from her expression he is correct. Her eyes answer 'yes'.

'You didn't tell on me,' she says. Her words hold a note of gratitude. 'That old man. You saw me, and you told him you didn't.'

'No, I didn't tell – he's my grandad.'

Grandad! Max suddenly remembers.

But he and Alex are no longer alone. A man appears at the storeroom door, his face livid as he spots the girl.

'You! Ya filthy tree-living hippie!' he bellows. 'Get outta here! How many times do I have to tell you to stay outta my store?'

The storekeeper makes a dash for Alex.

'Run, dummy!' she cries, grabbing Max's hand and pulling him with her.

—

Outside, Winston is hurrying towards the Pawn. The crowd of youths have moved across the car park and have surrounded his car. He steps between the youths, some of whom lean against the door, spotting graffiti in large yellow letters down the side of the vehicle. However, he chooses to ignore the 'art', open the door and get his goods – the now full bottle of water and the C cubes of protein – into the vehicle.

—

Max instinctively runs towards the Pawn and Grandad, but Alex tries to drag him towards the opposite direction. The store owner is on their tail as Alex tries to wrestle her hand free from Max's.

'The buke!' Alex shouts, and it works. She has his attention.

'Yes, I took it. Ok.'

The man is advancing on them, hands in the air, furious.

'Bloody tree-hugging hippies. Good for ...'

'Tonight – meet me where I first saw you,' she pleads.

Max lets her go.

'I'll give the buke back then,' she yells as she runs.

Max only realises the store owner is upon him when he grabs his arm.

—

The gang surround the car as Winston starts the engine. This time he appreciates the low purr of the car starting. *Where is the boy? Where has he gone?* he thinks, panicked and wondering where he should start looking. However, creamy pink goo lands with a thick splash against the front window.

One of the youths has painted the front windscreen with a smoothie, blocking Winston's view. The Model 1 instantly cleans the glass and the burst plastic cup rolls down the bonnet.

Winston feels a flare of rage inside himself and explodes out of the car door. But the instant he sees Max, this rage subsides. Instead, he leaps back into the driver seat and hits the accelerator with what remains of his rage. The rear wheels spin and the car skids, separating the youths like a frightened flock of birds.

Winston sees Max in the grip of the store owner. Max pulls away, but the store owner holds tight. Before Winston can straighten up the car, Max stops struggling. His face becomes a mask, and he appears to just ... relax. He raises his hands to the man's cheeks, and with a quick jerking twist, he spins the man's head to the side, forcefully breaking his neck.

Winston watches the man's body as it appears to turn fluid between Max's hands and pours limp onto the concrete – as if emptied. The gang members freeze, watching in horror, and they shrink back as Max appears to run towards them. The boy suddenly dives through the open rear window of the moving Pawn, and Winston steers the vehicle out of the exchange car park at speed.

Winston looks back at they pass the car park from Main Street and the youths have vanished. He sees the store owner's legs as they twitch. He hopes he will live.

Grandad heads for the mountain in silence. Home is calling louder than it ever has previously. The old man can hear it. His home in the rock is not far. And he prays.

He only starts to pray aloud when he spots the Law Patrol vehicle, driving behind them. It would be hard to miss the big hulking black and gold truck. However, the roof lights remain unlit, and Grandad hopes rise, and he tries to remain calm.

Then a screeching, *Wo-oor!* The siren on the Law Patrol car lights and spins. Winston grips the wheel tighter, his knuckles turning white as he depresses the accelerator. Like approaching jousting knights, the patrol car increases in speed and fury and gains on them.

Grandad shouts at Max, keeping eyes on the approaching threat in the rear view mirror.

'Get down! Duck down!'

The patrol car gets closer. Grandad's eyes dart about, his mind working through their options. The officer gets closer. Grandad discards five ideas. The truck gets closer, and Grandad has two options left. They may work. The siren light is so close, its lights reflect flashing across Winston's face. He decides. He has one idea that will definitely work, but it requires a sacrifice. A hard one to make. One he does not want to make.

Then the Law Patrol passes the Model 1. Winston can hardly believe it as the Patrol continues at speed, moving further and further into the distance. Winston watches, releasing his breath, hardly daring to loosen his vice grip of the steering wheel.

'Keep down until we get back into mountain roads. Ok?'

Max slips into the footwell and curling into a ball, closes his eyes.

Winston drives.

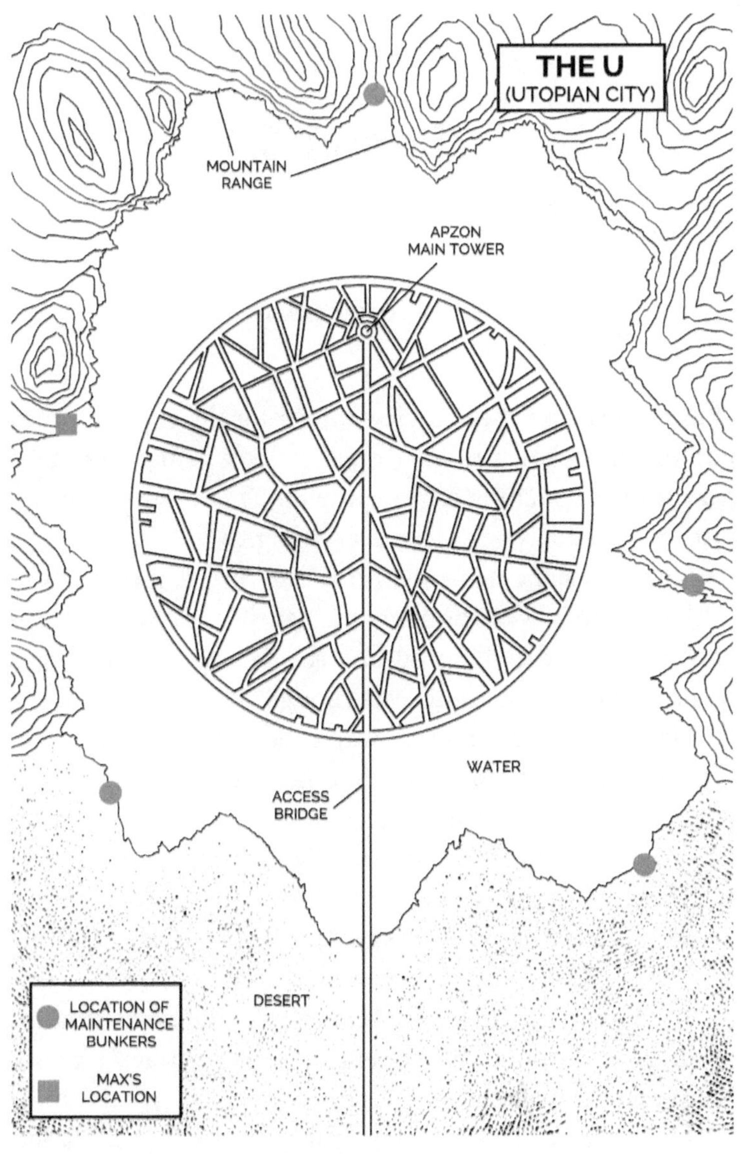
THE U
(UTOPIAN CITY)
MOUNTAIN RANGE
APZON MAIN TOWER
WATER
ACCESS BRIDGE
DESERT
LOCATION OF MAINTENANCE BUNKERS
MAX'S LOCATION

Chapter 6

A Stranger Calls

Winston watches the rear view mirror for the entire journey home. He looks away only once to look at the little boy. Maybe he is searching for the little boy. The events Winston just witnessed have changed everything.

He slows as he nears the turn. The turn is merely a gap in the treeline. Winston veers the car off the road between two trees, and they descend into the darkness of the forest. Winston knows the route even though there is no road.

He stops in the hollow where he conceals the Pawn. Grandad turns off the engine, but there are no words spoken while they sit for a while.

Grandad gathers the new supplies as he gets out.

'We need to get home.'

Max doesn't respond. He remains in the footwell of the car, staring at the floor between his feet.

'Max?' says Grandad, hoping to shake the boy out of his daydream. He pulls the passenger door open as he passes but proceeds towards home alone.

Max observes a white patch of skin on the back of his left hand. It's right where the pigeon pecked at him. He pushes against the whiteness with his finger until it turns pink. He unfolds himself and emerges from the footwell. Standing beside the car, he notices the stain on the rear seat again. He is drawn to it. He opens the back door and leans closer to smell the cushion.

He notices the ornament dangling on the rear view mirror for the first time. It's still swaying from the journey. It is a piece from a chessboard, a pawn. In broad daylight, Max realises that it is crudely shaped by Grandad. He reaches into the front seats and unhooks it. He takes a second to admire it before shoving it into his pocket and leaving the car. He starts pulling the tarp over the top, making sure it's hidden from sight. He doesn't know why he has to be so careful. Nobody ever comes here. As he fixes the tarp around, he circles the car and sees the yellow graffiti for the first time. The word, *NIGGER,* is spray-painted along the side of the car. He touches the paint and finds it's still tacky.

Winston can feel the effects of a day in the sun. He remembers how he burnt his first week in this place. He was Michigan boy, and his skin was not ready for Nevada sun. Max was born and raised here. But he lives in the shade of the old service bunker. He has never been out in the sun. This unforgiving sun. Winston thinks of rain. He remembers it and thinks about seeing again. He'd love to feel it on his skin again. It has been too long.

He considers rainbows. Rainbows are the sky remembering rain. Just like he is now. The sight of one of those colour-filled arches might quench the thirst he has for rain. Winston reaches the doorway, and looks back out across the lake. He realises Max has never seen a rainbow.

The old man prises the bottles free from his backpack as Max arrives in the door behind him. Winston moves to conceal the alcohol he's purchased with half of the credit. Max leaves his shoes by the door.

'Did you get any C?'

He waits for the old man to answer.

'Of course, that's what we went for. What else would I have bought?'

Max's eyes glance towards the cabinet beneath the sink, where Grandad has just hidden the alcohol. The boy knows Grandad will leave it there until tomorrow and then hide it where ever it is that he goes every day.

Max fills a pot with water. The water boils, the soup cooks, and Grandad busies himself chopping leaves. Max sits on his bed and pulls the curtain around for privacy. He reaches down into the front of his pants for the paper bag, pausing briefly to listen for Grandad. He's can still hear him, chopping at the table.

Quietly and slowly, Max pulls the stubbornly noisy paper bag from his waistband. He opens the bag, eyeing the chocolate inside, curious. *What is it? What does it taste like?* He looks up to check the curtain is fully closed. He hears Grandad whistling a tune in the kitchen on the other side of the sheet.

A sudden loud noise comes from the door. It's the sound of someone knocking on the door of the bunker, a sound Max has never heard before. Max parts the curtain to look at Grandad. Winston is mid-stir, spoon in the air. He places his index finger against his lips, and uses his hand to silently wave Max back behind the curtain. Max pulls the curtains shut and slides under the bedcovers.

Winston's whistling stopped the moment he heard the knock. His heart beat hard. Have they found him? Have they already heard someone inside? Is it too late to run? A male coughs impatiently on the other side of the door. Winston realises he is getting old. How did he not hear the man approach?

The caller coughs again. It tells Winston the caller has heard him and is growing impatient. Winston has no choice. He opens the door cautiously, looking over the young man standing there. The large black and gold truck that overtook them on the road is parked behind him. The man is sharp-faced, taller and broader than Winston, and muscular with black, glossy-wet hair. The angular edges to his face are as hard as the battlements of a stone castle. He wears the uniform of an enforcement patroller.

'Hello,' says the man as he steps forward, intending to cross the threshold of the bunker without waiting for an invitation. Grandad stands his ground, even though the inspector is now in his face.

'Officer Hitchcock,' says the man as he deftly steps around Winston. And just like that the stranger is in the cabin. The man observes words Grandad has carved into a piece of wood hanging inside the door.

Céad míle fáilte.

'You know there are no outside languages allowed here,' Hitchcock announces. 'Bad enough we're still using English.'

He jabs the sign with a gloved finger.

'It's this type of disobedience that has slowed down the transition to full binary.'

Grandad shakes his head in apology.

'Bad habits. They're often hard to break.'

The man uses his gloved hand to remove a warning citation disc from his pocket. He places it on the kitchen table.

'Sometimes they are quicker broken when we are reminded of the consequences.'

He peels off a grey leather glove.

'Old habits? How old are you anyway? How old must you have been at the selection? You look a million.'

The patroller is looking at Winston suspiciously. No one over the age of 30 was selected to enter the program. Winston knows his wrinkled skin gives him away.

'Life out here ages you quickly I guess,' Winston lies. 'The sun maybe.'

'Life out here?'

The patroller eyes him curiously. Winston is living far from the city.

'You have chosen to do so, have you not? You're one of the strikers, yes? The ex-workers from APZON Tech?'

Grandad nods even though he never worked at APZON Tech and is not one of the original technicians which Hitchcock presumes him to be.

'You people are a constant pain in my neck,' says Hitchcock. 'You don't live with the others?'

Winston doesn't answer. He is relieved the patroller believes he was one of the striking labourers.

'It certainly is not easy to find you out here, hidden in the woods.'

His voice changes tone.

'As if you are trying not to be found.'

Hitchcock, whose name is branded on his shiny breastplate pin, moves around as he chooses with no regard for Winston's home. He steps around the room, eyeing and inspecting everything except behind the curtain.

'And you?' the patroller smiles, finally taking his eyes off Winston's possessions. 'What department did you work in?'

Grandad walks to a drawer in the kitchen and produces a small metal identification pin. It's two inches long and the width of a pencil. He hands it to the patroller without making eye contact.

The patroller plugs it into a device in his hand.

'Says here you live alone?'

Hitchcock paces up and down the room while reading Grandad's file from the screen.

'Yes.'

Hitchcock looks at Winston and then directly at the two coats hanging beside the door.

Max is listening to everything under the bedcovers. Hitchcock takes his eyes from the two coats and glances at the curtain pulled around Max's bed.

'Alone? Indeed.'

Hitchcock no longer paces.

'How old are you again?'

Winston hoped his age wouldn't come back up, but Hitchcock's eye is suddenly distracted. He has spotted something far worse.

'You play chess?' says Hitchcock, staring at the board in the shadows on the floor.

Max holds his breath behind the curtain. A knife of fear cuts through him. How foolish to leave the chessboard out. Grandad told him not to, and now he has doomed them both. Grandad and he are sure to be found out.

Hitchcock hunkers down beside the chessboard on the dirt floor. Then using his gloved hand, he swipes a single pawn from the game.

'Just a way of passing time for me,' says Winston.

Hitchcock closes his hand around the pawn.

'Really?' he asks, and he rises to his feet.

'Have you been tempted by the prize money? Win a round of the tournaments? All you hippies are the same. You say you hate commercialism, money, power but when it comes to it, given the chance, you'd take the money as fast anyone else.'

Hitchcock squeezes the pawn and smiles.

'Hippie should stand for hypocrite.'

'No,' Winston replies. 'No interest in that.'

'Really?' Hitchcock sneers. 'To a refugee like you, one would think it offers a lifeline to a better place.'

He tosses the pawn into the air.

A better place? Winston raises an eyebrow.

Behind the curtain, Max looks out from under the blanket and spots the crumpled paper bag sitting at the end of the bed. It will bring trouble upon them if it's spotted. On one elbow at a time, he crawls across the bed. The bag is open, and he can see into it and see it does not contain chocolate.

'Gotcha!'

Max freezes with fear behind the curtain as the angular-faced man catches the tossed pawn with satisfaction. His fisted hand clenches around it hard.

Hitchcock walks across Grandad's path, still rolling the pawn back and forward on the palm of his glove. Winston steps out of his way. Hitchcock appears to be leaving, and Grandad reassures himself he only needs to hold back a little longer. Hitchcock stops in the doorway. He stops beside the two hanging coats and his eyes move mockingly from the coats to Winston.

'There has been an incident, a robbery, at a small convenience store in the city.'

Hitchcock stands in the open door now, speaking back into the bunker.

'A car came up this way, but it vanished off the road not far from here.

'You don't have access to one of the APZON vehicles, do you?'

Grandad shakes his head in silence.

'Very well.'

Hitchcock extends his gloved hand to Grandad.

The clasping of another person's hand in your own is a custom Winston remembers as an old-fashioned show of respect from a life before. The act is outlawed. Hitchcock waits with his hand extended. Grandad's hand has been tucked in his pocket in a fist. He intends on leaving it there, refusing to fall into the man's trap.

At that moment, Max's movements to hide the paper bag cause a blanket to slip from the bed and slump to the floor. Both men see this from the door, but Winston grabs Hitchcock's outstretched hand and pumps it enthusiastically. The patroller's eyes drop to inspect Winston's hand in his own. His pupils dilate as he sees the back of Winston's hand.

'No scar!'

With furious force, he grabs Winston and shoves him towards the forest floor. The old man's face touches the dirt.

'And you don't show up on location.'

Hitchcock kneels over the old man, twisting his elbow behind his back, out of its natural alignment.

'All The APZON strikers have the scars of their tracking chips ... or they show up on location sensors.'

A strand of slicked wet hair falls and swoops across Hitchcock's forehead.

'Reason enough for suspicion ... possession of outlawed items? And now this? Aren't you an interesting one? You're older than your papers say too. Who are you, and how did you get here? Why would an old drunk and refugee nigger live out here?'

Grandad does not open his mouth to speak. He breathes heavily through gritted teeth, refusing to let the man take anymore from him.

'Legal refugee status or not – out here, alone in these woods, you could vanish, and nobody would ever know.'

Hitchcock takes the pawn from his pocket, and holds it in front of his own face while keeping Winston twisted in place on the dirt forest floor. Taking the chess piece, he places it's round tip inside the old man's ear.

He raises the gloved hand at a height above his own head, directly over the pawn. He smiles with the sadistic anticipation of forcing it into the old man's ear. Maybe it might pierce his brain.

Max hears the men outside. He looks into the bag, confused. There is no chocolate like the girl said. Instead, the bag contains a phone. Or is this a 'candy bar' like the girl said?

He leans closer to the curtain, and with two fingers, pinches a pleat and pulls it a little to one side. The low evening sun fills his eyes, but then his pupils adjust. Hitchcock's hand never reaches the pawn. The bullet sends him flying off Winston, ripping a hole through his uniform and stomach.

Winston turns to see Max at the bunker entrance. Hitchcock crawls, desperate to put distance between himself and the mystery shooter. He crawls across the dirt, face down towards his truck.

Winston scrambles to his feet.

'No!'

His tries to wrestle the gun from the boy, but the grip is immovable.

'Max let go.'

But he doesn't. Max's eyes are like Grandad has seen them before. They are not angry or calm, happy or sad. They are just fixed, floating weightlessly.

Winston blinks and lets go of the gun just as the gold-trimmed door of the patrol car opens, and he sees Hitchcock pulling out a gun of his own. In an instant, Max knocks the patroller to the ground and stands over Hitchcock's fallen frame, his rifle pointed at the patroller.

'No!' Grandad pants on the ground, feet away from Hitchcock.

'Max! Don't kill him.'

Max pauses.

'Max, I've spent your whole life teaching you not to kill. Showing you. You don't have to. You still have a choice ...'

But Max stands in place, pointing the rifle and questioning if he has a choice. He feels his forefinger flex as he pulls the trigger and then blinks as he only hears the click of an empty barrel. Grandad struggles to his feet unaided, and grips the rifle barrel. Max allows the gun to pass into the old man's hand as Hitchcock's eyes cloud over. The patroller succumbs to his injuries anyway.

—

Inside, they sit on the edge of Max's bed. Winston stares into the distance.

'That man was going to kill you,' says Max. 'Was it because of the chessboard?'

'Partially.'

Grandad continues to stare into nothingness.

'He had other reason too,' he adds.

His head turns to Max.

'You stopped him. Thank you. But it was wrong to kill him, Max.'

'Why?'

'Why? Thou shalt not kill! For all the reasons I've been trying to teach you. Because life is precious, and you especially need to understand that ...'

Winston sighs and pulls the bed covers back for Max. He covers the boy's lower half.

'The shopkeeper. In U City.'

Winston watches Max as his eyes close. He thinks of how close he has held him. Years of holding him tight. In a day, has he lost his grip on the boy. In an irreversible way.

'Max?'

But not an unfixable way.

'I need you to tell me you will never take life ever again. And I need you to mean it. No living thing.'

He watches the boy falling asleep, knowing he has work to do before the sun comes back up. Grandad whispers to the sleeping boy.

'Sleep. Rest. I have something I have to show you tomorrow. Something I cannot put off any longer.'

Then, in a timeless way that everybody has held someone, the old man holds Max.

—

Max wakes, unsure how long he has slept. He tosses. He only hears Grandad snoring.

He pulls the covers down from over his face. It's still dark. His secrets are starting to build. Once Grandad and he had no secrets from each other. It's still dark, and he's still wearing his clothes from the day before.

Max's leg trembles, and pulses run through the flesh, a feeling he has never felt before. Something is happening. Max puts his hand to the sensation and realises it's the phone. It has been hidden in his pocket the whole time he has slept. It hums and lights up the whole room. Max quickly covers himself and the phone with the blanket; underneath is lit up like a bright, white igloo. He reads:

FROM – U News Daily.
SUBJECT – Daily updates for citizens of the U.
Unite-Unify-Utopia
FROM – APZON Delivers.
SUBJECT – Stock delivery of C-protein today at ...
FROM – APZON Weather.
SUBJECT – Sun forecast for this week, next and the foreseeable
...

FROM – APZON THE TOURNAMENTS
SUBJECT – Another player qualified this week for the tournaments. They will begin competing ...'

Max's thumbs move about the screen for only a moment before he sees the game. On the left top corner of the home screen, a small image of a pawn, inside a sandy-coloured square.

The tile draws Max's finger towards it, and in he goes. A chess board appears onto the screen ...

'Welcome challenger ...'

—

The phone twinkles a chime at midnight. Max is thinking about her, when a message appears on the screen. Max touches it. He listens for Grandad as he reads.

'The forest where we first met. Tonight. Alex'

At three minutes after midnight, Max swings his legs off the bed, ready to sneak by the old man. He doesn't have to. Grandad is gone. Not in his bed. Not in the room.

Max pinches his shoes, finger and thumb, then stands up softly. Slow, he creeps towards the door.

This is not a good idea.

Max can hear the old man's voice inside his head as he leaves. The cold night touches him outside. He zig-zags through the trees; through the forest, glancing back often. The moonlight streams down through the tiny gaps in the overhead trees. It appears and vanishes, appears and vanishes again, on and off as he slips through the shadows.

—

The bunker door opens again sometime later – just a crack. Well, a crack big enough for a man. Grandad edges his way out through the opening, trying not to wake the sleeping boy who isn't there.

—

Leaves crunch under Max's feet. His hands are fists inside his pants pockets as he walks through clouds of his breath. The moon above the treetops pours down upon a broken blanket of leaves. It lights up a wide area ahead. The moon has drawn a circle on the forest floor like a spotlight that's nearly ten feet wide.

The leaves crackle underfoot, but he hears noise in the trees around him. Noise brings a fool's comfort to Max like the wool wrapping a wolf might wear before a sheep. A noise in the darkness of a forest is scary. Silence in the darkness of a forest is scarier. He stands in the moon's spotlight, looking up into its face.

At least I'm not alone.

He walks on until he reaches the boundary line. The far side of the forest – a line he has never crossed – looks the same as his side. Max steps near the laser line. *What if the message is intended to lure him here?* Before he can fully process that thought, there's movement. He squints, peering into the far side.

Is it her? What if it is something else? He is being foolish. Out here in the middle of the forest. This far from the cabin – from Grandad. He is alone. What if someone is there behind those trees? What if someone sees him? Grandad has spent as long as Max can remember keeping him hidden, and now he might undo all that in an instant. The crunch of a leaf, and she appears from between two trees. But then vanishes again between others.

Is that her? Did he see something? There she is again. She moves in and out of his sight as she gets closer, and then she is gone again. She steps out from behind a trunk beside him. Two feet from his face on the other side of the laser line. She is within touching distance behind the impenetrable barrier.

'You came,' she says. 'I didn't know if you'd be here.'

She steps closer and holds out her hand to him. Max watches as she reaches out to him and glances at the sensor on the nearby tree. Fearing her limb will be reduced to ash, he reaches out across the sensor to stop her.

He wonders if he'll ever touch anything with that hand again and hopes it is worth it. Now, as he reaches her hand, he thinks it is. His hand has passed a line that he has spent his life behind. And his hand is holding hers. The sensor never makes a sound.

Suddenly, self-conscious, he drops her hand and stuffs his casually into his coat pocket.

'It's ok. This sensor doesn't work,' Alex smiles.

Max realises the tree trunk where the sensor hangs is damaged, exposing the pipework inside the tree. He pulls his hand from his coat pocket and shows the phone to Alex.

'This is yours. You put it in the bag at the store. I need to get my book back from you.'

'You brought it here?' she says. 'They're probably tracking it now. You shouldn't have brought it with you.'

'But it's yours.'

She looks directly at him.

'It's not mine. It belongs to APZON. We can destroy it now. I just needed it to load the money onto.'

She climbs a fallen tree trunk, her arms wide for balance as she moves along, touching her heels to her toes.

'Money?' Max asks as he watches her. 'You were stealing from that shop?'

She stops and smiles.

'I only loaded the money on the phone ... you stole it from the shop.'

Max looks around the forest floor and inside himself.

Alex jumps down from her beam.

'Don't sweat it, kid. Like everything else in the store, it's owned by APZON. They can afford to lose it and ...'

She glances back over her shoulder before she yells: '... THE MISSION IS – TAKE DOWN APZON!'

Body-less voices echo the word 'APZON'.

'Actually, we should probably destroy that thing now. No doubt they've tracked the network for the coins on it.'

She holds out her hand for the device.

'But,' Max looks longingly at the phone. 'There's a game on it I like.'

'Show me,' says Alex taking the phone from Max's hand and recognising the Tournament App.

'Ah you play? You any good? We all tried at one stage or another to win that bloody thing.'

She taps on the phone's screen.

'It's ok. The game remains, but the credits are gone, and it can't be tracked now. You can knock yourself out. Just don't tell anyone how you got it.'

'I don't know anybody except my grandad,' replies Max.

'You don't know anybody else?'

'No.'

'You're telling me you have never met or seen anybody but your grandad? In your whole life?'

Alex looks him in the face with disbelief.

'Well ... you,' he says, softly.

'I knew there was something weird about you... something weird about how that old man ...'

'There's the book ...' Max interrupts her. His mouth fails to consult with his brain before words come out. Max is eager to return to the subject of his book.

'The day we met. My mam's book.'

'Yeah, I remember. That's what you call that thing?' she asks.

He nods.

'It's important to me.'

'The things inside it, the stories, wizards who grant wishes and big sewn-together men who are dead and brought back to life,' says Alex. 'My dad has read those to us. I don't have it. My dad has taken it off me.'

'What?' Max is appalled. 'I need it back!'

'You can come back with me, and ask for it yourself. He has questions of his own that he'd like to ask. We all do.'

The phone chimes suddenly in Alex's hand.

'Holy shite!'

She reads the screen, and shock registers on her face.

'Maybe it's a good thing we didn't destroy this phone, kid. There's a 980 score on the tournament on this thing.'

'The tournament?'

'You don't know the tournament either, do you? You are a weird kid. The game you said you are playing, that's part of an online league.'

Max's interest is piqued.

'A monthly competition with a prize of the winner's choosing, with no monetary limit. Funded by Skinner's own money. You play chess?'

'Yes.'

Alex registers his confidence and certainty.

'Kid, did you score the 980 on the phone?'

'Yes,' says Max. 'But there is a problem with the algorithms, not so much a problem but a ... manipulation. I'm sure I can score better with another try. I ...'

Alex impatiently interrupts Max's rambling.

'You've done this on your first try?'

He nods.

'You fancy yourself as a challenger?'

She looks from Max to the screen beneath her thumb.

'You planning to win a one-way ticket to dreams come true?'

Alex walks away, scrolling.

Max hesitates to follow. Watching the sensor, he pushes a single toe forward across it. Nothing. No laser. No heat. No blast. *She's right; that one doesn't work.*

He follows her from a distance, watching her. He sees she's getting dangerously close to the sensor on the next tree over – one Max has every reason to believe is working.

'What are you doing?' Max runs towards Alex as she kneels inches within range.

'Listen, kid,' she says, looking up at him. 'I know you're weird and all, but there's a really high score on this phone. I don't know if you or someone else has put it there. But if this score stays on top of the board when this month ends, they're gonna want to speak to whoever's got it. They'll come after this phone.'

She holds the device up.

'I don't want it.' Max says, suddenly frightened.

Turning her face away, she lobs the phone past the sensor.

It's blasted with a bright blinding light. The phone hits the soft forest bedding with an explosion of sparks, its length newly adorned with a smoking crack.

Alex sighs with relief.

'Where did you learn to play chess?' she says.

'From my grandad.'

'Of course,' Alex smiles. 'The grandad.'

Max is quiet for a moment before responding: 'and I think from my mam too.'

'Your mam?'

'She owned the notebook.'

'Notebook?'

'The notebook. Book. Journal. It was my mam's.'

'Was?'

'Yeah. She's dead,' says Max. 'She was a research scientist. She kept notes on stuff. Stuff she considered important. My grandad says those stories are the ones she wants me to read. I think they're supposed to have lessons in 'em.'

'How did she die?'

Max blinks. He has no idea.

'Well, I'm pretty sure she's dead,' he says. 'Grandad never says it and talks about her like she's still alive. But I can't … feel her. I just think she … he wants me to believe she's alive, writing me stories that he says are hers; things that are supposed to guide me through life as I grow up.

'But I can see it in his eyes. I think he writes the letters, her stories. I do. But I slip the loose pages in her notebook and pretend. For his sake.'

'My dad read 'em to me. I like one.'

'What is it about?'

'A scientist. A lonely … guy who brings – who creates a monster. While trying to find a way to bring people back after death.'

Alex starts to back away and then turns, walking deeper into the unknown side of the forest. And then, she's gone from sight. He catches a glimpse of her from behind the trees much further in, and then she's gone again.

'Are you coming to get your stories back?' he hears her cry.

Max looks back in the direction he has come; in the

direction of the cabin, towards Grandad, towards what he knows.

The moon is still bright and the night sky is dark. Smoke whisps from the phone at his feet following some draught between the trees.

Max decides to follow, his steps quickening until he can see her ahead on a barely discernible trail. He sees she's following two other figures. Max stays slightly behind, watching. One of them, the biggest and tallest, turns and looks back at him.

'This is him? Doesn't look like much.'

He has the beginnings of a more mature shape than the others – more muscle now than Max might ever have. However, the stranger's boyish cheeks suggest he has not yet lost all puppy fat. His hair is black, and now – in the dark forest at least – so are his eyes.

'Yeah, Nat, and looks can be deceiving,' says Alex. 'We know that.'

Max looks at the taller boy assessing him and feels something he's never felt before. Instinctively, he lowers his eyes as he walks. He feels self-conscious.

'He scored a 980 on the game, Nat.' says Alex.

'In The Tournament?'

Nat sounds shocked. He yanks Alex's arm, and an animated exchange begins between them, words that Max cannot hear.

Max looks at the third person, wondering if it is a boy or a girl. But the figure is slight in body and probably the same height as himself. It makes him or her the smallest in the group.

Max admires the figure's heavy brown hair that swings in a curtain that conceals their face. Max really tries hard to catch a glimpse of the face, but then the person suddenly addresses him in the darkness.

'What wrong with your hand?'

The voice belongs to that of a boy. Max quickly conceals the white patch on hand with his other hand.

'Nothing.'

'What's wrong with your skin?'

'Nothing is wrong with my skin. I just had an incident with a ...'. Max does not know what a pigeon is called. 'Nothing wrong with my skin.'

'It's ok,' the boy replies. 'I'm sorry. I'm Thackeray.'

Max realises the boy is apologetic because of his defensive reaction.

'I'm Max.'

Thackeray looks with curiosity at Max's hand again.

'It's kinda like you're half one thing and half another. I feel like that sometimes. Do you have those patches all over?'

Max shakes his head.

They walk in silence for a while as Alex and Nat walk ahead, heads close together in deep conversation.

'That thing Alex brought to our camp – is it yours?'

'The book?' asks Max.

Thackeray nods.

'Yeah, it's a book,' says Max. 'Well, a journal. But stories. Same as a book.'

Thackeray lights up at the mention of stories.

'Sam has read us the one about the Frankenstein.'

'The monster,' nods Max, paying more attention to the two ahead than Thackeray by his side.

Thackeray studies Max's face rather than the forest ahead or where he walks.

'What's a monster?' Thackeray asks.

Max thinks.

'Something with no soul.'

—

The four walk further into the forest. Max can see the others are familiar with the terrain and where they are going. And what they head towards.

—

The path is climbing, winding and rocky. It is also wet, slippery in parts and breath-taking in steepness. They duck under tree branches, shimmy down rocks and clamber up boulders, moving higher and higher.

The air gets colder, crisper, brighter, and the air gets thinner. A new, different type of air than Max has known before is filling his lungs. The first dark glow of the rising sun lights the clouds, painting them a tinge of warm pink as the four climb through cold mist. Max takes Alex's hand climbing up and offers his while climbing down. Nat's eyes are still black. Thackeray is silent. He has not spoken since his earlier curiosity about Max's hand and book.

Alex stops Max with an upturned palm. She turns her back to the mountain trail, letting Nat and Thackeray hike up ahead. She steers Max by his elbow and through an opening in the trees, he looks down upon the city from this vantage point. The first traces of the morning across the sky helps him pick out the silhouettes of familiar places from a new perspective. He can make out the lake, deep black in the darkness, and knows just where home is, knows where Grandad is, in the back room in bed. Peaceful.

Max looks back to the U City. It is even larger than he thought. He sees the spike, the store, the car park and for the first time, the whole city he has lived so close to.

Just yesterday, the store was the furthest he has ever been from home. And just the day before, he had never been away from the lake. He sees the road, straight and perpendicular like an artery through the town to the APZON Citadel at the centre.

'My mam worked there.'

'Your mam worked at APZON?'

Alex's voice registers shock, but Max nods.

'Was she with the first to come?'

'I don't know.'

Max feels the answer is somehow wrong.

'Was she with the protesters?'

Max shrugs, hating himself. *Why doesn't he know these things?*

'What protests?'

'You really are living in a box, aren't you? Mass protests by APZON workers, years back. Hey, you ever think your mam had other notebooks, paperwork?'

Max can hear distant sounds at the top of a mountainside.

'Yeah. I mean no. I've never thought of it before. But might make sense.'

Max looks out at the Citadel but is distracted by sounds again; familiar sounds, out of place. A hollow banging of wood against wood, voices, a distant peal of laughter. He follows Alex up over the hill where Thackeray and Nat have disappeared.

Then he spots where the sound is coming from. The slope levels off to a wide, flat area near the mountain's very top. He can't see where Thackeray or Nat have gone, but in the first dawn light, he can make out people and huts made of wooden boughs and branches. Wooden buckets and tools and cold fire pits are strewn round the huts. He can hear the sound of a stream running nearby. This is a village within the forest, atop the mountain, built into the nature, with people living off the environment.

Alex holds out her hand to him with a beckoning smile. As they walk between the huts, the people look at Alex first with familiarity, then at him, in surprise. But he watches surprise turn to anger and fear, and he feels fear himself. But Alex just keeps nodding, smiling and walking on. Determinedly, she leads him towards a hut in the centre of the village.

A thick, heavy blanket hangs across the entrance. Alex pushes it aside and slips under. Then holding it back again from inside she waits for Max to join her. Max doesn't. Glancing back up the village where they've come from, he's nervous. He knows nothing about this place, nothing about these people, nor how safe or dangerous they might be.

He looks back at the small camp, and considers the entrance to this hut and the darkness inside. The moon is fading behind the increasingly pink sky.

'You want your stories back or not?' Alex says.

Then her face is gone and the blanket has dropped. He lifts the blanket and follows her in but is blinded by the darkness until his eyes adjust. The walls are woven branches and the ceiling above him, within reach, is leafy. The space is small, maybe 12 feet at its widest, and has no discernible shape. A candle lights the whole hut.

He sees a long, flat bed near him and another at the back, both raised inches off the soil floor. A man sits in the bed furthest from him. This man's rugged face is stubbled, scarred by life but still striking and handsome. His hair is blonde and shoulder length. He is the same colour as Alex, not like Grandad. Caucasian, but brown; a mixture of dirt and sunburn. His head remains bowed, reading as he sits cross-legged. It's only as Alex lights a second candle from the first that the man peels his eyes away from the page and sees Max. He closes the book instantly, abruptly, but Max recognises it. The feeling the book gives him comes back.

The man rises to his feet fluidly. His linen shirt has sleeves longer than his arms. He's also wearing shorts but no shoes.

'This is the boy?' he says, standing with his face inches from Max's. He glances at Alex but fixes his eyes back on Max's quickly.

'I told you I would get him to come,' she replies to Max's surprise.

'Where'd you get this? Where'd these stories come from?' the man demands.

Max takes a step back.

'My grandad. They're my mam's. But my grandad gives them to me.'

The man pulls his weight to his back foot and looks distrustfully at Max.

'Your mam?'

His brow has narrowed.

Max looks at Alex then nods his head.

There is a tense and silent stillness in the hut that lasts seconds but seems longer.

'Yes, a long time ago,' says Max.

He looks nervously around the hut.

'It doesn't feel like that long ago,' says Alex's dad.

He holds the book behind his back.

'I'm Sam. I'm Alex's father.'

He returns to his bunk, leading Max under one arm.

'Your mam was one of us. An APZON employee.'

He sits once again cross-legged and Max joins him. Sam flicks through the pages of the book, leaning nearer the glowing candle flames.

'Your mam always told stories like these,' Sam says, gesturing at the pages. 'I should have known. You look like her.'

'My grandad says that too.'

'I recognised some of the stories as soon as I started to read. She liked these. Not just the stories but their meaning. I remember her telling them like they were weapons during her speeches.'

'Speeches?'

'What do you know about your mam?'

'Nothing that I am certain of anymore,' admits Max.

'Your mam was the head of the Science Research and

Development department at APZON. I worked near her sometimes in the factories. She'd come there sometimes.

'She didn't like the way Adam used her research. We all came here to build a promised new society. She foresaw the true direction that society was taking. And she felt the original Utopian vision we were sold was never really the goal. He was using us all.

'She felt that everyone – all the people who walked away from their lives, societal rules and laws to follow a tech-genius into the middle of nowhere and build a perfect, fair and just world – deserved to know the truth.

'So, she led us. She started the revolution against APZON – the failed revolution. That has us here, like this. Not wanting – or able – to fuel APZON and unable to return to the homes we once knew.'

For the first time, Alex sees a glimpse of the man her father is.

'The relationship between a father and his daughter is unique. Similar to the bond between mother and son, I'm sure you'd ...'

Sam reconsiders.

'Your mam talked about her dad a lot.'

'Grandad.'

The word prompts Max to scramble to his feet. He can see beyond the curtain that it's getting brighter outside.

'I have to get back home. My grandad he'll be ...'

'She missed him a lot,' says Sam.

Max hesitates. Confusing words spring from Sam mouth.

'He was the reason she regretted coming here. He wasn't

allowed come. No matter how close a relationship she made with Skinner. He would never allow a man of that generation come. Really, I think it broke your mam, leaving him behind.'

'Leaving him behind, where?'

Max forgets about the dawn once more.

'Leaving him behind to come here. To build U City, the Citadel. The new and perfect civilisation,'

'My grandad is here.'

'Who is telling you that, Max? They are lying to you. Be careful who you trust in here.'

'Nobody is telling me! My eyes tell me. I live with him.'

'Nonsense!' says Sam, getting to his feet too.

'Your grandfather would never be allowed here. How old would he be? Part of the agreement we all made in coming here is to leave behind everything that generation – those generations – built.

'He'd never be allowed passage. He would bring with him a religion, ideologies. Hell, they're halfway through destroying the language he speaks. They would never let someone so contaminated breach this world.'

Max is bewildered about the things Sam says.

'I have no clue about anything you say, but I'm telling you,' he says, 'my grandad is at the bottom of this mountain. Asleep. In the home I've lived my whole life in - with him!'

'It's true, Dad.'

Alex speaks up for the first time.

'You've seen him?' says Sam. 'I'm telling you there is no way a man or woman of that age from the old ways and old life would be allowed anywhere near here. Skinner won't allow it.'

Max lifts the curtain, and the first fingers of dawn fill the silence.

'Are you certain the man is who he says he is?' says Sam.

'Dad, his grandad is old Alcoholic Abe from the supply store,' says Alex. 'I've seen them together.'

'Alcoholic Abe is Sarah Turk's ... Alcoholic Abe is your grandfather?'

Now Sam is confused too.

Alcoholic Abe? Max is forced to confront his many questions about Grandad's drinking.

'I have to go,' Max says. 'If I'm not at the lake before he ...' He stops.

'Wakes?' says Sam. 'You have to be home before he wakes don't you?'

'Yes.'

'You haven't told him you're here?'

'I have to get back.'

The curtain drops behind Max. Alex steps to follow him, but is stopped mid-step by her father. He holds her by the hand.

'He came for this. Be careful,' he says, passing the journal of Dr Sarah Turk to his daughter and releasing her hand.

Outside, Max doesn't get far. He's handed a large triangular-shaped sail by a group of village children, and he's excited, intrigued and distracted all at once.

'You are the people in the skies. I saw you once. You move through the sky. I know I saw ...'

Alex catches up with him and takes the wind sail from him, smiling.

They both duck as another sail passes over their heads. The children scatter and run, every second one holding a similar sail with a different pattern. Laughing, pointing and kicking up dust, they run into the darkness of the nearby trees.

'They're going up to the rock to fly them in the sunrise,' Alex says, pointing above them. 'Do you want to try?'

Max cranes his neck back, and looks in awe at the overhanging rock that juts out of the mountainside soaring above them.

Alex smiles as she sees the familiar sight in new eyes.

'If you jump at just as the sun breaks the horizon, it feels like you are flying; leaping into the sun. You can close your eyes and pretend you're crossing the horizon and going outside of this place.'

'Outside of the board,' says Max.

Alex looks off the mountainside. Taking some time before she speaks, her eyes fix on the horizon.

'My whole life I've felt like I am trapped. Inside something I am too big for.'

She turns to face him.

'You ever feel like that?'

Max nods his head – seeking to find what she has been gazing at on the horizon.

'In chess, if a pawn makes it to the far side of the board untaken, it can become any piece of its choosing,' he says.

'But it goes back on the board,' says Alex. 'It must stay in this game. There is no escaping the game.'

'What is a pawn outside of chess?' Max asks.

He is unable to even comprehend an 'outside'.

'I wanna find out. I want out of this place.'

Alex has never uttered this aloud before. She has someone she can tell this to for the first time in her life.

But Max is distracted by the increasing light.

'I have to get back before my grandad wakes.'

He moves to go, but she beckons him in the direction the children run, a path between the nearby trees.

'If you wanna be at the lake before sun up, this is the quickest way down.'

And she darts away and disappears between the trees.

Max looks back down the mountain trail, at the path which has led him there. Then again, out at his and Grandad's lake from this new height. Finally, he looks at the space between the trees that this magnetic girl has just vanished.

'Wait up, Alex!'

Chapter 7

Into the Unknown

The path spirals uphill through the trees, and he emerges onto a vast flat rock above the village. It stands like a tongue jutting out of the rock face. Here, the wind pushes across the rock face, and Max feels its strength. It wages its strength against his entire body's length, blowing into his face.

Max expected to see many more children here. He saw so many come this way, but he turns and looks around at the handful on the rock. Where the rest have gone? One of the children runs across the flat rock, a sail above her head. Max catches his breath as he sees this small girl run straight for the edge. With her sail stretched above her head, she throws herself off the edge and drops out of sight. Max runs to the edge after her.

Twenty feet below, he sees her sail and her skim the treetops, down the mountain slope, descending further and further. Max looks back for Alex. She is busy with a small boy, helping him bind a cord onto his wrist; a cord which attaches to the sail he holds above his head.

Max searches the boy's eyes with a curious need, but the child's eyes never meet his. They're fixed to the horizon.

Miles away, out of reach of any other person here. The sail passes almost under Max's chin just as the previous did, and the boy is gone. Looking over the edge, he watches the top of the sail follow some invisible line that the little girl has left in the air.

Alex is holding another sail.

'Sounds like your mam was a real rebel,' she says.

'Maybe,' Max responds. 'Your dad knows more about her than I do. I just wish I could have the chance to talk to her. I have so much to ask her.'

Alex ties cords to the wooden struts of the wind sail.

'All the adults in our village worked at APZON until the protest. She led them out. My life looks the way it does because of her. I have questions I want to ask her too.'

'What did they protest against?' Max asks.

'The shady shit that Skinner started to do with the technology they'd help build. Technology he was still asking them to maintain. Things that they did not sign up for.'

Max looks back blank-faced. He doesn't understand any of it.

Alex takes a deep breath and exhales with exasperation.

'APZON is a technology company. It gathers information on people, through social media and stuff like that. But everybody, well, most tech companies have been doing that, so no biggie. Things like what people like, dislike, the words they use, how they speak, what they look like, how their voices sound, their tone, their opinions, thoughts, education, everything. They know people better than people know themselves.'

She explains all this as she binds the sail cords to her wrist.

'APZON has amassed so much information, it can tell what a person thinks before a person thinks it, knows what a person would say before they say it. That's pretty shady and weird right?'

'Yeah.'

Max can only see the passion she has as she explains.

'Well, here's where it gets really shady. Skinner, or APZON, start to build artificial intelligence or A.I. versions of people. The A.I. programme works just like the person, sounds like the person.'

She throws the sail over her head and onto her back.

'When a person dies, their family can contact this A.I. version of their dead loved ones communicating with them with emails, texts and even video calls with their lost loved ones.'

Alex looks straight into Max's eyes.

'But if the family want that communication to continue,' she points an accusing finger at the empty sky, 'APZON charges a subscription!' Fucked up right? APZON owns your loved ones after death.'

'Yeah ...'

'Messed up,' says Alex, emotion welling in herself. 'They own the person. If APZON could put their programme in a physical body, they'd charge a subscription to exist. Imagine a life whose existence is reliant on the software running it. It has no choice but to subscribe. And no knowledge or memory of an alternative.'

Max's breathing quickens.

'They could be self-conscious or self-aware? Are the memory files conscious? People in their own right?'

Alex shrugs, but Max shakes his head.

'It can't be right, not morally. Why hasn't someone tried to stop him?'

'Because he's too big – get over here – too rich.'

'What?' Max watches her grip tighten on the long wooden strut with both hands.

'Sorry, please come here,' she says, pointing at a spot right beside her under the sail. 'He is too big, too rich. No one has the money or power to take him on. But all the APZON staff, my dad, everybody, probably your mam too – wanted nothing to do with it.'

Max crawls under the bar of the sail and holds it like Alex does.

'Many of them went on strike. You ready?'

She pushes the bar forward at arm's length, pressing the sail against both their backs.

'So what did he do? Skinner?' Max asks.

'Fired them all,' she says. 'Without being able to earn any money, my family and the others moved to living ... like this. In the trees.'

Her eyes darken with feeling.

'But still determined to stop Skinner and APZON.'

Max's eyes wander out off the mountain.

'Ready?'

'For what?'

'To run.'

Alex is running so the sail belts Max on the back, shoving him forward. He recovers quick, steps forward again, and he's running. He is running for the edge of the rock face. After which, there is nothing but falling.

His breath disappears as he and Alex drop. He feels he lost his heartbeat somewhere above their heads. The temptation is to reach up for his breath, his heartbeat, for safety, for something, anything to hold. Instead he tightens his grip to the bar of the wind glider and thinks of his mother. He tries to picture her face, of what he wants to say to her. The light hits his pupil and instead of falling, he realises they are moving forward and out, over treetops, in the sky.

They cut across the treetops like a bishop zipping across a chess board. He gasps involuntarily. Every muscle in his body is rigid, and his hair flies behind his head. The knuckles of his hands that grip the sail bar get colder and colder. He thinks about the billions of possible chess moves. He thinks about how APZON has a history of people, of staff, of everyone including his mother. APZON has enough information on her to build a version of his mother's mind. One he can talk to.

His mother's pages, the stories he has read and knows so well, float in the air under Max's feet. Instinctively, he feels the giant paper pages hold his weight, ink staining his feet. The paper holds him as he skims the tree tops, the air above the trees. His mother's pages and words, the only contact he has ever had with her, carry him, as the glider rains her words like pixie dust as they sail across the sky. The words are declarations of lessons learnt from a life who no longer lives.

From somewhere distant he hears Alex squeal. He hears the giant duelling bishops' swords clang beneath him, but even they pause to watch as he and Alex soar over their heads. The black knight gallops beneath his feet like an arrow, and the Tin-man and Lion stop to look up from where they stand by the lake. Black and white.

Something changes; his mother's pages, which have borne his weight, flutter away from beneath him and briefly, he feels his heartbeat rise again. He feels tree leaves whip his leg.

Max looks at Alex for the first time since they have left the rock face. She screams with delight. Max watches as she pulls herself up, threads her legs over the bar of the glider and sits perched. She looks below, between her legs, or straight in front of her and reaches to grab one of the cords which hang down over her head.

Max follows, pulling his own weight up to sit as she does and watches. Alex tugs a cord with force, and Max feels the glider drop on that side. His hair pulls back off his face again, and the breezes warms slightly. He recognises the rocks below and now, trees too. He eyes the lake – his lake – up ahead as Alex guides their sail, up, down, left and right, missing tree branches with inches to spare. The treeline ends suddenly, and their reflection swims under the surface of the water as they fly across the lake.

They are quickly running out of height but not water. Max looks over his shoulder. Their air cuts a V-shape shadow in the water's surface which gets bigger and spreads further behind them. With a forward jerk and a loud splash, they hit the water.

Then all at once, his ears fill with water, his breath leaves, cold embraces him and he's below the water's surface; looking up from the other side of a mirror at the sun in the sky.

He soars up and the water's surface peels down off his face and shoulders. He snatches a loud breath and punches his arms about, flailing in the water. He calms as he hears Alex laughing.

He watches her crawl on her hands and knees across the muddy bank, dripping water from all her weighted clothing. She manages to drag the glider out of the water behind her.

'That was awesome!'

Max hears her revel as he ploughs through the water and drags himself to the lake's side. She squeezes water from her snaking hair as Max emerges from the lake, wringing out his heavy clothes.

'Home by sunrise,' Alex smiles. 'What did I tell you?'

Taking a moment, he smiles too. It's a different smile from hers.

'Do you want me to get you some dry clothes or a towel?'

'You don't have time,' says Alex, shooing him towards his cavern of a home. 'Go get in there before your grandad realises you're gone.'

She holds the glider aloft and winks.

'It'll be a long walk back dragging this thing. I'll be dry again before I'm home.'

Max watches Alex go, but then he remembers.

'Alex, wait!'

'My mam's book. My book, my mam's journal. I forgot to get it from your dad ...'

Alex remembers and peels the wet journal from the back of her waistband. Sorrow-filled, she shakes the sodden book twice.

'Sorry about that,' she says, handing it over. 'It's salvageable. Just keep it by the fire and it will dry out in no time.'

Max holds the dripping book with two fingers and then begins to pick and peel the pages apart with focus.

'Wait,' he says as he finds the pages he's seeking. He passes her the pages.

'Bring this back to Thackeray. I wanna loan them to him. Just one night cause I wanna keep all the stories together. But tell Thackeray to read it. Please.'

Alex reads one word, Frankenstein. She folds the damp pages and tucks them in inside her top. Her voice rises as she walks away.

'I'll bring this back to you tomorrow,' she says, and she is gone between the trees and out of sight.

As he peels his soggy clothing from of his body, he hears someone in the forest nearby. Crouching, he notices the patroller's truck is gone. It's no longer parked outside.

Max watches as Grandad steps out of the trees down river. The old man walks briskly towards home.

—

The sound of the lapping water soothes Winston. He is almost back. He hopes the boy won't be awake yet.

Alongside the lake, he notes, curiously, the surface is rippled and disturbed. Behind his back, Max steps behind the door and into the house.

—

Max feels Grandad's warm hand on his shoulder. Even through the blanket, it still radiates his heat. His clothes are hidden in a wet pile under his bed. He feels the large hand rock him back and forward.

'Come on, sleepyhead, time to get at it. I've already one cup of coffee gone.'

Winston clears his throat. He has lied to the boy his whole life. Why now does it feel different?

'I have something important to show you today, remember.'

Max turns over and looks at the old man with eyes that crave sleep.

'Be right there.'

He rolls himself from the bed and carries the desire to burrow back into it to the kitchen.

Winston slumps at the table as Max passes behind him. Noticing the absent smell of coffee, Max pours the last of some water from a bottle into a pot, and then places it over heat. He sits opposite his grandad.

'The water is on ... if you want a second cup of coffee.'

—

Max wakes to the sound of the water boiling and bubbling. Jumping up, he turns down the heat, takes the coffee and powdered milk from the shelf over the counter. A spoonful of coffee goes into Grandad's cup and one spoonful into the other.

He replaces the powder on the shelf and carefully fills the cups with boiling water. He stirs both, tastes one, then remembers to turn the bags around – the APZON label must remain unseen. Grandad insists the label is always faced away from sight. He leaves Grandad's cup on the table in front of the old man's nodding head.

—

The smell of the coffee remains in the air as they get ready to leave. Winston pushes the door out, and instantly the cool shade of the cabin is a contrast to the hot day outside. The sun has risen, and the stillness and silence outside is almost oppressive. Grandad closes the door, sheaths his knife and shoulders the strap of rifle.

Max thinks about his new friends as he plods alongside Grandad, his hands tucked into his pants pocket. He wonders if he can call them friends. Do they consider him a friend? The thoughts pass through his mind.

But then Grandad stops and rubs his palms together. He is standing on the lake bank near the cabin. He checks he's in the right spot, looking over his shoulder and down his outstretched arm, measuring by eye.

'M7:26, You remember where we always start from?' Grandad asks without noticing his query remains unanswered.

Max looks on, tired. Winston looks one way then the other. He looks up at the mountain peak then straight ahead into the forest. Winston's turns to face the breeze. It lifts his hat. He catches the peak, pulls it down and nods to Max.

'Are you ready?'

'I don't really know what to be ready for, Grandad,' Max answers, feeling his hand itch in his pocket. The patch of white now larger.

'If this were a game of chess?' the old man says as he leads them on, 'What would you be ready for?'

'Everything,' says Max behind the old man. 'If this were chess, I would be ready for everything. At first I was going to say the gambit, the way you attack. But then I realise when I play chess I prepare for all other possibilities. So, I'm kind of ready for ... anything.'

Winston smiles while shaking his head.

'No, not everything.'

The old man looks up at the sky, longingly.

'There are still rules to the game. Limitations to the pieces' movements, 40 squares no further.'

Max looks for what the old man is looking at above. He sees nothing new.

Probably Mother Nature, he thinks. The spaces between his toes feel still wet, and the wind picks out damp parts in his hair.

'Grandad, can I ask you a question?'

Winston pushes on determinedly through the trees.

'No questions, Max. I need you to pay attention today. I need you to remember the way. Remember the locations.'

Max continues to hold the question he has already held for days. He stays close by the old man, but finds himself lagging behind at times, thinking about chess or Alex or Nat or Thackeray.

'Come on, keep up the pace,' says Grandad as he marches on.

The sun is high as they journey. Their shadows collect under their own feet. Max watches for patterns as they wind their way through the forest towards the 'something' Grandad leads them towards.

—

Patterns lie everywhere; patterns in the trees, in the path beneath their feet; in the wind's sound and the spaces between the trees. Patterns in the moss, mud and gravelly stone beneath their feet. Max sees patterns in the rise and fall of the forest floor. Up and down, rolling but always keeping the trees' roots buried beneath.

The bark on the trees conceals more patterns. Max holds patterns in that space behind his eyes, the place where his mind is; the place he goes when he plays the game or as he moves through the forest.

—

They go around a large tree, Grandad leading. Max's eye is drawn to the foot of the tree. It has no bark. It's not a tree, he realises as he examines its smooth and shiny black surface. He looks up its tall length. It's a cylinder of some sort. The top of that shiny pole remains concealed in the trees from this close. He brings his chin back down from his inspection and runs to catch up with Grandad.

Winston is determined to keep moving, but Max's head is turned by another strange forest shape. This is wider than the last one he saw. This is smooth and shiny black too but in a massive solid block with a giant horse's head on top.

Grandad pays no attention to this either.

Twisting, turning, Max realises these figures are all throughout the forest, hidden about and forming patterns. He walks amongst the lost pieces: a towering high white bishop, another lofty black rook tower, a shorter, solid elephant. He walks through the history of the game, through the patterns and now – although he is behind – he no longer follows Grandad. He feels he knows the way.

'We're here.'

Grandad stops, like Max knew he would. Winston readies himself for something, unslinging the rifle.

'Grandad, what is an alcoholic?'

Max feels the silence.

'Where have you heard that?'

'That's what people call you, isn't it?'

Max sees the weight that word holds displayed on Winston's face.

'People? What people?'

Winston is startled, recalling all his efforts to keep this boy hidden.

'Alcoholic' was Alex and Sam's word. Max couldn't say where he'd heard it.

'That man, the patroller who came to our home. He said it. I heard ...'

'No Max, he called me an old drunk.'

Max is sweating.

'He was just trying to provoke me to react.'

Grandad fills the silence now between them and elaborates reluctantly.

'An alcoholic is a person who ... is addicted ... or cannot stop drinking alcohol. Even when it has bad consequences.'

'Alcohol? That's your drink.'

Winston hesitates.

'Yeah. That's Grandad's cold tea.' He clears his throat. 'It's OK to drink alcohol. It's just not good for you to lose control to it … drink too much.'

Max takes the weight of the rifle as Winston hands it to him.

'Looks like now is the right time to show you this place. I wondered if you were old enough.'

Max watches as the old guy bends and begins feeling around in the fallen leaves on the forest floor.

Hunched over, he moves around until finally he grabs and pulls something free from under the layers of forest debris. It's a rope, which it rises scattering dirt and dusty into the air. It's tied to something beneath. Grandad leans back until the rope becomes taut and holds the old man's weight at an angle.

Grandad grimaces as he pulls, and the ground moves. Or a section of it does. A wide board covered in forest bedding moves across the forest floor as Winston pulls it like a sliding door. A dark hole beneath opens.

Max watches his grandad continue silently. The old man sits at the edge of the hole and then proceeds to lower himself into this long rectangular slice in the ground. He drops completely from sight.

Panicked, Max drops onto the leafy forest floor and peers over the edge.

'You coming?' he hears from somewhere under the forest floor.

Max looks at the rifle that his Grandad has left on the forest floor and makes a quick decision. Then he dangles his legs and lowers himself reluctantly into the darkness, still gripping the ground above him. Then there's light, and he drops to land inside. The light continues to move about, flickering as Grandad moves about with a torch. From under here, Max can see it's a far bigger underground chamber than he expected from above.

As his eyes adjust, he squints at what appears to be a table. But Grandad's voice calls out for him. The old man is about fifteen feet away in the darkest end of this rectangular domain. As the torch flits about the space, Max's eyes sees the bunker for what it is. It's easily 20 feet wide and seven deep. There is enough space to walk, but much of it is filled by one hulking object. There's only room to circle the edges of the central relic this hole conceals. A black car fills the central floor space. He's never seen a car like this. It must be many decades old, but it looks pristine.

Max reaches out to touch its glossy surface.

'Max!'

The boy jumps and yanks his hand away from the cold metal body of the car. He can't resist sliding his finger along the body of the vehicle as he walks towards Grandad's voice in the darkness beneath the forest floor.

The car sits higher as he approaches Grandad. He feels the vehicle rise beneath his hand. He hears the sound of metal, of clinks and clangs. Max makes out shelving along the back and far side walls. Then the tomb lights up with the woof of a flame hungrily feeding on fuel and oxygen. Grandad holds a lantern, twisting a small wheel on the base.

'A 2015 Mustang,' says Grandad lifting the lantern and gazing at the car with a mixture of pride and admiration.

The two front wheels are slightly elevated, and propped up with two metal tracks. Max thinks the tracks must have been used to lower the car into this underground cave. Max runs his fingers over the symbol on the front. It's like a silhouette of the knight piece from the chessboard.

As Grandad lifts the bonnet, the engine looks like no other; a jigsaw of failures. Pipes and hoses run in and out of vacuumed glass bottles. Max sees still-new engine parts discarded around the floor.

A small table and chair is pushed against the back wall under shelving. Wooden shelves hang top to bottom on the other wall. The shelves are stocked with the most amount of bottles Max has ever seen in one place. Empty, half-empty, three-quarters full and everything in between - all bottles which contain or contained alcohol.

'Max,' says Grandad, his voice dry. 'If anything ever happens to me, I need you to hide here. Do you hear me?'

'Why would anything ever happen to you?'

Grandad looks at the boy. He has practiced this speech but has always avoided it. He regrets it now.

'It wouldn't. It won't. But I need you to be safe in case it does, and I don't get back.'

'Get back from where? Where are you going? To work?'

Winston takes a deep breath.

'This is my workplace, kind of. This is where I come every day.'

'This is where you get Mam's stories? And Mam's flowers?'

Max looks around the space inside the underground bunker.

The old man's eyes wander before he answers.

'No. Well, yes. This is the place where I spend the day, and this is where I need you to hide tomorrow.

'We'll bring a few days supplies with us when we come back. I just needed to check if anybody has been here.'

'Why do I have to stay here? Because of what I did to the old man at the store?'

'No, Max, that's not why.'

'Why? Because I shot the patroller? I didn't want him to hurt you. He was going to ...'

'No, Max, that's not why either.'

Max wonders if Grandad knows about him drowning the grey creature. That was an accident. He was lost in his daydreams and in that frightful first sighting of Frankenstein.

Frustrated, Winston snatches a whiskey bottle. He yanks the cork, but as he raises it to his lips, he stops. He lowers the bottle.

'Remember you asked me about alcohol? And the patroller called me an alcoholic?'

Max nods.

'I'm not an alcoholic, Max. People in town think I'm an alcoholic because I buy so much alcohol.'

Winston holds the lantern above the roof of the Mustang.

'This thing has a 3.8-litre petrol engine. The minute it starts, their emission monitors are gonna know about it. But I'd love to hear it.'

'I don't understand, Grandad ...'

'This thing runs on something called petrol. That's a liquid we've damn near run completely out of it. If I were back home, I could just go to a local gas station. But, here it's not that simple. They don't sell petrol here.

'So, I've been trying to get this thing to run on alcohol – or any other type of liquid available here for that matter. I'm close, real close, I think. But it doesn't matter now.

'So listen, Max. That patroller? When his patrol vehicle isn't docked at its station tonight – the end of shift, they're gonna wanna know where it is. The location tracker will lead them right outside our bunker. So we can't wait any longer. I have to go get petrol. So we can finally try to get out here.'

'Where are you going to get the petrol? I thought they don't have that here.'

Winston beckons Max to end of the bunker and directly under the opening they came through. He points up at the sky and the smoke trails above.

'You see that? Skinner has everyone here fooled that this place is run on clean energy. But I know that when he got here, it didn't work. Why I don't know, but it didn't. They're burning something, old-fashioned fossil fuels and selling it as clean electric. There's no smoke without fire.'

Grandad's finger points to the sky as evidence again.

'They're burning something. And I know the smell of burnt petrol. There's something added to it, but they've got petrol. Enough of it to run a city. That's where I'm going tomorrow.'

Winston walks back to the engine of the Mustang.

'I'm close. I just need more time. But now we don't have that time.'

The width at the centre of all our hourglasses is fixed though the speed of our sand flow is never the same. Heavier sand falls quicker.

The old man points at the side of the car.

'Petrol goes in here.'

Then he hunkers down, and with the lantern beside him, looks underneath the car.

'There are bull bars on the front. I have welded them straight to the chassis. So this thing shouldn't have to stop for anything ... once it gets going. The problem is getting it going. We have enough fuel in the tank for maybe an hour's drive. But no more. And we need a lot more.'

'What am I supposed to do? I don't know how to drive, Grandad.'

Winston has felt this fear before and has always tried to ignore it in the past. He realises how stranded they are. Why would anyone encourage someone to run from an oasis in a desert?

'You won't have to. Just come here and wait for me.'

The old man thinks fast, pinching the bridge of his nose.

'But just in case, I can show you here how to drive.'

He pulls a door.

'Get in.'

Max sits into the seat, closing the door as quietly as he can. Grandad hurries around to the other side.

'Max, you won't need to drive anywhere. Just stay here until I come back, but you're right. You should know how to drive.'

–

Nineteenth-century driving explained, the two shut the car doors. The lantern is starting to struggle as the sun, which earlier poured through the opening, is fading. Winston takes a bottle from the shelf, causing Max to look away.

Max looks around. The table is dust free. So too are the implements on top of it. He notes a stack of eight or nine journals (red the same as his mother's), a pen, a candle and an object unknown to him. And a box of bullets, four rows of four casings. The first row has three bullets missing. He steps closer to inspect the unfamiliar item. It's a small block of wood with a pivot lever on its back and a black button pad on top. A wire trails from it off the side of the table.

Max pulls the chair out from underneath the table and sits. While Grandad is distracted, Max slides that last bullet from the first row into his pocket. He'd lost that other bullet. He will be certain to not lose this one. At eye level, he can see a scattering of ugly chess pieces: failed carvings that have not made the cut. Carved, failed, burnt, failed, familiar – close but wrong.

Winston is busy topping up the lantern's fuel with alcohol. He uses the brighter light to illuminate the car, leaving the boy in the shadows. He talks almost to himself.

'The bars on the front are strong enough to force the wall on the way in, and I think they're still pretty solid, though they did take a whacking.'

He studies the front of the car.

'I think they still have another thump in them. Enough to break the wall one more time ... as long as they haven't reinforced the wall.'

Winston's forehead wrinkles as he thinks out loud.

'I haven't been out that far in long time. And nothing in this place has stayed the same. So we need to make sure we have enough fuel to really hit it.'

But Max points at the wooden block with tiny metal see-saw on top.

'What's this?'

Grandad turns the light, and for the first time sees Max at the table, the table of search.

'It's a Morse code receiver.'

The old man has long hoped that his search for escape will not be passed down a generation.

'It's for sending messages. Or hoping to receive them.'

'How can this send messages?' says Max, touching the simple block.

'It's getting late, Max. We have to be getting back before the sun is down and it gets cold.'

Grandad is searching around in every direction.

'But how does it work?'

'You see that page stuck against the wall in front of you? That's a Morse code alphabet and tells you how to spell your message with dots and dashes.'

Max barely has time to see the code before Grandad says they must leave but not before instructing Max to extinguish the lantern.

'We can't leave that burning.'

Granddad lowers an arm to pull Max out into the evening above. Daylight has very near run out of patience.

Max squints into the trees as Grandad covers the bunker hole. The pieces, towering in Max's minds-eye, have all moved position in the trees. The board is different now; the patterns new and constantly changing.

The giant marble knight now looms next to the concealed bunker. A Mustang overseeing a Mustang perhaps. A marker for when it is needed.

Grandad turns to see Max's hands are empty. Where's the rifle?' he asks.

Max lowers his head preparing to lie. 'I left it down there,' he says.

The knight's pupil-less, marble eyes glare down on him from under a disappointed V-shaped brow. The giant knight pays no attention to Grandad. And the old man returns its disinterest. Grandad squints out into the forest, listening for a change in its silence.

'Probably the best place for it.'

Winston's utterance triggers a clamorous fluttering near them as a pigeon takes off into the air. Shedding grey feathers, it flies off into the treetops.

Winston looks up between the trees at the sky passing and sees the dust cloud float in the wind overhead. In the dim evening light, it sails past the moon's spotlight like a swarm. He can smell it in the air.

'Let's get back home. Back to the cabin. Did you blow out the lamp?'

Max nods.

He follows the old man, thinking of the hot smell by the lake the day before. Looking back, he sees the knight stand sentry, guarding the secrets beneath the forest floor.

Must not forget this place if anything ever happens to Grandad, he thinks. Max hopes he never needs to remember.

His mind wanders as he walks behind. He rubs the back of his hand again and notices another white section of skin, further up the same arm.

The old man walks the whole way with his knife drawn. The large chess pieces disappear as he moves further from the Mustang's place of rest. He's surrounded only by trees and cube-shaped water pumps back in the known forest.

—

'Grandad, why are there pipes inside the trees?'

Max has been wondering about this since he spotted the pipes.

'How do you know about those?

'There is a damaged tree, a bit back.

Winston feels a reluctance to answer, a reluctance he doesn't know the source of. However, admiring Max's curiosity, he does.

'Some of them do – not all of them. The tall trees in this forest aren't real trees. They aren't natural; natural grown. That's why I don't like the sight of them.'

'What are they for? The ones with pipes?'

'The taller trees are absorbent. They capture the carbon-mono ...'

Winston stops.

'They catch a gas that the little trees give off.'

'Why?

'For the water. Trees need water. And there's no real water here either.

Max looks quizzical. He's no better informed.

'The tall trees absorb a gas and send it through the pipes to the city. There it's mixed with ... It's mixed. And water is made. The water supplies the city because people need water too, and the rest is pumped back to water the smaller trees. And the process runs like that – always circulating.'

Winston notices his pride has dissipated since last he explained his process.

'Woah, that's pretty clever!'

'Thank you.'

It's an instinctive response; a youth-learnt politeness. However, he feels a small piece of pride in his work return; probably more than he felt before the eyes of the investors.

But the feeling is cut short with Max's next words.

'Grandad, my mam is dead, isn't she?'

They hear a rustling sounds in the trees to the right of where they walk. In an instant, both Max and Winston drop lower. The rustling stops just as sudden.

Winston wonders if it's another pigeon. And how did it get here?

Grandad unsheathes his knife while scanning the treeline. Max's mind is racing.

What if it's Alex? What if she steps out from behind the tree and Grandad reacts? Or what if it's Thackeray or Nat. He can't let it happen. He will have to stop Grandad.

The trees rustle again, and Winston positions himself to pounce if necessary. The bushes shake longer than before. Winston flips the knife around in his hand as something or someone gets closer. And then closer. Then it's here. And both stare breathless as out springs a head from the leaves.

'Grandad,' Max speaks low.

'Hmm.'

The old man doesn't move.

'What is that?'

There is a silent moment. Max watches the 'thing' as Grandad's unblinking eye brims with tears. The sight reminds Winston of the day he crashed through the perimeter wall and how long he's been living here. It also reminds him it has been a long time since he's seen living animals from the world outside.

'That,' the word causes a tear to trickle from the rim, 'is a camel.'

It's Lumpy…

Grandad lowers the knife amazed that the creature has made it this far …

'A what?'

'A camel. It's an animal. They are animals, I mean.'

Lumpy has hoofed it well beyond the perimeter wall now. He has seen so many new things along the way. Someone has built Utopia; a society designed by a tech-trillionaire. And Utopia is close …

Max looks at the camel in wonderment. It's like a knight or the horse on the Mustang, only larger. It's huge and ugly and lumpy; brown hairy skin wrapped tightly around different things at once; one of them a knight. It might be soft to touch if it weren't matted in filth.

'They? There more of those?' whispers Max, stepping closer.

The forest undergrowth crunches underfoot, and the camel's head swivels with fright. Its eyes fix on Max, and it leaps into a bounding run. They both watch as it corners on its ankles, zig-zagging counterintuitively three times. It vanishes from their sight behind some heavy foliage.

Then noise and light. Loud and bright.

Max knows the sound – a cracking and fizzle pierce through the air with the red sparking flash.

'No!' cries Grandad, running.

They follow a braying grunt behind the bushes. Grandad reaches it, but stops, stepping carefully, in a crab-like fashion, nearer.

Max walks back the trail path until he can see around the trees. Grandad crouches lower as he nears the smelly beast. It lies on its side, kicking, wailing. The old man kneels, and inches nearer, slowly, until he's beside the dying animal.

Laying one hand on its stomach, he feels its rise and fall beneath. He places the other behind its ear, rubbing downward to the animal's shoulder. Winston strokes the animal soothingly over and over again, feeling the rise and fall of the camel's breathing slow under his other hand.

Grandad watches his old and wrinkled hand pass, up and down, over and over again. He watches the pain with hate, and he waits. Lumpy sought his own Utopia. He wonders if he can make it.

Max can see the smoke, still wisping black from the device on the tree. The camel got too near the laser-line. He watches his Grandad kneeling beside the camel. The old man strokes its neck rhythmically. Max feels the hand as if it were rubbing him; a little boy remembering a lifetime in his grandad's hands. Touching, holding, hugging, carrying him. He has grown and the old man has gotten old. Time passes.

Grandad waits for it to die, but still it brays in pain. Max has to go back. He cannot let its pain linger. He sets off running through the trees. He needs the rifle. He races through the dusk to find it. Grandad hears and then sees Max running back up the trail they've come. Running like life depends on it.

Where on earth is he going?

Winston's attention is drawn back to the labouring creature.

Max finds the rifle easily. It hasn't moved from where he's hidden it. He finds the bullet in his pocket, needing it sooner than he expected. He runs-jumps-skips and ducks through the trees back to the struggling creature. He has to end its pain. He stops as he hears something approaching on the trail. Panting, Max struggles to silence his breath.

It's Grandad who walks up the trail towards him. Max sees the old man behind the sight at the same time as Winston realises the rifle is pointed in his direction.

Max points the barrel at possible danger. At ... Grandad. He does not lower it. Why? An instinct out of his control.

'Thou shalt not kill' and all the other lessons, morals and tales and stories and lies from his grandfather's mouth pass through Max's mind. He sees the sight-cross adorning Grandad's body. Max can see it there, but Winston feels none of its weight.

Max holds his position, and for a moment, between heartbeats, nothing moves.

—

Grandad's eyes are closed. The kaleidoscope of colour sprouting from the pupil behind his eyelids is familiar.

A wind cuts across the lake and rattles the bunker's door in its frame. It's twilight and the sun creeping over from behind the mountain paints a shadow along the face of the treeline. The lake, door and mudflat in front of the bunker door is glowing orange in the last of the daylight.

Max steps out from the darkness of the trees, his shirt stained dark and glistening, coated in blood shoulder to shoulder and neck to waist. He no longer has his coat, and he strides proud and empty-handed. Lost in thought, Max fails to notice the patrol truck.

The patroller spots Max before Max sees him.

'Excuse me.'

The sudden voice stops Max reaching for the door.

'The register shows one citizen inhabitant living here. An elderly man. Who are you?'

Max recognises the voice. He replies calmly though his heart is racing.

'He lives here.'

Max turns to see Hitchcock. He is strong, healthy and standing two feet in front of his eyes.

'I'm just a ... friend.'

Hitchcock removes that leather glove.

'Friend?' he says, almost accusingly.

'Well then, maybe you can help me, friend.'

Max waits, but Hitchcock does not appear to recognise Max.

'I am looking for a chess player.'

'A chess player?'

'Yes.'

The gloveless hand slips inside his jacket, and he produces a digital reader from a pocket within.

'A game of chess has been won on a device last used at this location. Right at this lake. Yesterday.'

Hitchcock looks away from the screen and takes a moment. He watches the stillness of the lake water in the wind.

'Now I need to find whoever played such an elegant game,' he says.

'You'll have to ask the old man about that when he gets back. He'll be here any minute.'

Max buys some time.

Placing the device back inside his jacket, Hitchcock nods.

'Yes, we just will have to ask Winston ... when he gets back.'

He eyes Max as he gets closer.

'The old man's name is Abe,' says Max.

'Of course ... Mr Abe Turk. I forgot myself. Must have gotten confused. Reading that wrong.'

Hitchcock smiles.

'Trouble with my wiring, maybe.'

Max retreats a step as Hitchcock approaches offering his gloved hand.

'And you are?'

The patch of skin on Max's hand itches.

—

Alex feels the blood build behind her face. She's sweating, breathless, tired and hurting, but she runs downhill, through the forest, vaulting fallen trees nonetheless. She feels the cool breath of air and knows she's getting closer to the lake.

She stops when she reaches the lake. She shouldn't stop, but she's mesmerised. What is it? What are they? And where have they come from? They are like nothing she has ever known. The place looks safe, so she approaches carefully. There is nowhere else as colourful in the entire forest. She knows because she has walked every inch of it. A rectangular strip of soil is marked out on the forest floor with a frame of small rocks close by the lake. The bed of golden yellow inside the rectangle is like a familiar dream. Tens of them, in bunches, each like tiny green trees but with tops, heads, faces may be the word, like tiny suns. Bright and yellow and beautiful. They look soft, and they are somehow growing up from under the soil, like the soil beneath her feet.

Do you remember your first time seeing a flower? She wonders what else might be under this forest. What is the forest capable of, if this?

Alex questions what she knows about her world. When has she last seen something new? The world is shifting. She bends down beside them. Their aroma meets her. Beautiful. Fresh. Alive. She reaches out gently to feel their delicate petalled faces.

'Get away from there!'

Alex leaps upright in fright, plucking a daffodil head as she does. She cups it in her hand behind her back.

'What are you doing at that? You shouldn't be at that.'

The angry voice comes from a blood-smeared man, and Alex runs.

She hears her breath hard in her ears and the forests leaves rustle about her as she runs. She smells coffee. She tries to look in all directions as she moves but crashes into her pursuer face first.

'Max!' she cries. 'Max!'

'What did you say? How do you know that name?'

The bloody-faced man grips her firmly by the shoulders.

'Max!' Alex yells, struggling. She knows his house is near. 'Get off me!'

He recognises the book in her hands: Sarah's journal.

'Where did you get that?'

No words can replace a mother, but they are all Winston can think to give the boy.

'That's not yours! Give it to me,'

Winston wrestles with the wriggling girl to snatch the book from her.

Alex smells his bloody clothes.

'Where is he? What have you done to him? Where's Max?'

She kicks out at Winston's leg, and wrenches herself free from his hold. She heads towards the bunker with the old man chasing. Reaching the rock inscribed M7:26, she runs towards Max's home, calling her friend's name in hope.

'Max!'

But Winston is still fast, and he manages to catch hold of her from behind just as she reaches his home. He's determined not to let her go this time. Not until he has answers

'Who are you?' he says breathlessly. 'How do you know that name? Max.'

Too tired to fight this time, Alex pants for breath but looks defiantly into his old face.

'Where is he?'

'How do you know Max?' he insists.

But she eyes him suspiciously.

'Whose blood is on you? Where is Max? What have you done to him?' Alex yells.

Winston lets her go to her surprise.

'Where is he?'

But Grandad walks away from her and into the space he has long called home. He emerges seconds later, scanning the treeline across the lake.

'He's, he's gone ...'

'A camel in the forest, it had somehow gotten in and ... it was wounded, and we ... I just thought ... Max ... He would have come back here.'

The old man goes to search inside again, and Alex follows.

'He's not here!' she exclaims. 'Is he alive?'

'Alive?' Winston says. 'Why would he not be alive?'

'You're covered in blood! I thought you killed my friend.'

Winston notes the term 'friend' with a surge of great joy.

'Young girl, this is not Max's blood. Nor mine. Do you want to tell me what you know? You can start with how you met Max?'

—

The day darkens outside, and their coffee-stained cups have lost their warmth. Alex feels at home in the bunker with the old man. Now the strangeness between them has gone, she admires the space. However, neither can illuminate the other on Max's disappearance, and they continue to wait, hoping for the boy to return.

'Do you play chess?' says Alex, spotting the chessboard in the corner.

Winston glances in the same direction.

'That's Max's. Yes, I play chess. But technically that's Max's now. I gave it to him. He has such a great interest in the game.'

'You taught Max to play?'

Winston shakes his head.

'No, actually, he taught me. I have never seen anything like how naturally he took to it. As if his genes have memories of it.'

'He's good. I've seen it..

Realisation dawns on Alex.

'Oh shit! I think I know what happened. They probably sent someone for him.'

Alex rubs her temple with two forefingers.

'The tournament ... Max must have qualified,' she says.

Winston watches her, puzzled.

'He qualified? He qualified for what?'

'I think I know where he is ... I know where he is.'

Alex leaps to her feet, knocking Max's chair behind her.

'His score. He must have won. They have sent someone for him ...'

'Wait! Who? Who has sent someone for him. Nobody knows he even exists.'

'Yeah, but he won.'

She can see Winston has no idea what she is referring to.

'He won the tournament! You don't know what the tournament is? A game of chess. Max must have won the online game. Skinner uses it to find the most intelligent in the city – where you win a prize and Skinner pays for the ...'

'Slow down. Tell me. An online game of chess?'

'Run by Skinner, APZON ...'

'Slow ... breathe ...'

'I knew it. I've never even heard of a 900.'

Alex is pacing now, speaking to herself.

Winston gets up and grips her by the shoulders.

'Tell me what's happened to Max!'

'Max scored a 900 ... I saw it – a very high score on this game. He scored it against an A.I. called Purple Rain7. It must have been enough to get him into the tournament rounds at the Citadel. They must have come here looking for him.'

Winston feels it all his years of care and caution start to unravel.

'No, Max doesn't have any way of playing an online game. Max doesn't even know what online is. Let alone have a device.'

Winston feels the girl's shoulders slump under his grip.

'I ... he had access to a phone for few hours.'

She swallows hard.

'I gave it to him. This is my fault.'

As her head drops, Winston wraps an arm around her.

'No, this is not your fault. This has been in motion from before your birth, Alex. It sounds like you are trying to help.'

He goes outside and spots the tyre tracks amid footprints in the mud. He was so busy chasing the girl and looking for

Max, he hadn't seen them before. Alex stands by him, facing the road into town. They watch the tyre tracks vanish on the hill's horizon, towards U City.

Winston turns to face the lake and watches the stillness on its surface.

'Do you ever wish you could go back?' Alex says.

'Not physically, I mean. I wish I could go back in time,' he replies.

He paces towards the rock, the marker for his home with the letters and numbers etched on it.

'I carved this verse into the rock on my first night here. Ever since my first night in this place, I've have the same dream. I'm standing on a large clock face, sweating, try to force the hands back – drag them back, push them, kick them. Nothing works.

'Then I'm standing still – heavy, paralysed – at the end of a tunnel and the whole world, and everything in it, is being pulled away from me really fast through the tunnel.

'Like the future is flying through the tunnel away from me. And all through the tunnel, the present plays out in images on the walls. Images like wet paintings, drying out to become permanent. Time, history is passing with each step, but the future is running too fast for me to keep up.

'I get to the middle of this huge tunnel. I feel tiny, insignificant, and after a certain point I can't see the pictures on the wall. Beyond a certain point, I have no idea what will dry on the walls of the present.

Winston looks into the lake and remembers the first night he arrived in U City. After smashing through the wall, he followed her detailed instructions. His gratitude after finding the bunker in the forest quickly turns to regret; he even considered the possibility it was all a trap. The thought, though brief, was enough for him to hate himself. He was ashamed that his opinion of his daughter might have changed and was laced with suspicion.

He remembers carving the letters and numbers into the rock.

'M7:26,' he says aloud. 'Matthew Chapter 7, verse 26.'

He sees Alex look at him quizzically.

'It's from an old book. A wise one. It says we should build on rock and not sand. Towers built on sand fall. This rock engraving will be here after both of us.'

Winston remembers waiting at the location, exactly where he stands now and seeing the Pawn's headlights come through the trees towards him. Then heavily pregnant and in tears, his daughter stumbled out of the Pawn into his arms. And there on the backseat, Winston lost his daughter. Death in one arm, and life falling into his other.

And standing beside Alex, he thinks how he may have lost that little life too.

Chapter 8

Inside the Citadel

Hitchcock steps from the patrol truck. He buttons one of his sleeve cuffs in the time it takes Max to step out beneath the towering APZON headquarters – the Citadel. Sand blows across his tennis shoes as Hitchcock shuts the patrol door behind him.

Anyone looking down from the glass windows above would not notice the boy. Max looks like an ant – insignificant compared to the might of the building. A Goliath overshadowing a child.

The building, APZON's epicentre, is a steel-meshed cylindrical cone, a frame, wrapped in a delicate-looking coating of smart glass. The building was designed to represent the human body – its skeleton and skin. Skinner has always sought to breathe life into his creations. Within the building's peak is an inverted metal cone, pointing downwards and containing much of the technology that powers the building. But Max cannot see this from where he's standing, up close, neck craned upwards in awe.

The majesty of the building continues to astound him as he follows Hitchcock into the building. The floor on every level is a circle of thick, reinforced glass; the circles decrease in circumference as the structure ascends into the heavens. Outside, the sun hits the building and reflects off it, dazzling those around it for miles away.

Max follows Hitchcock across the ground floor reception. It's almost empty. He sees two aluminium tubes, elevators, one each side of the lobby, running up the outside of the glass.

Max is so busy looking up, he almost trips over a small machine humming below knee level. Max reads the name Atlas VI along its hockey puck-shaped edge. He sees it's shining the floor and looking across the vast expanses of glass, Max realises cleaning is a never-ending task.

Hitchcock places his palm flat on a screen at the reception desk.

'Sign in here. Place your left hand to the pad and hold it for a moment.'

Max does so absently; he pays more attention to a small advertising screen flickering on the wall behind the desk.

Hitchcock waits.

'Try it again,' he barks.

Max repeats the action.

Hitchcock blinks. How can a citizen be unregistered? This must be an error. He hands Max a tablet and pen from the desk.

'Do it by hand – your first initial and last name.'

Max writes on the screen: 'M. Turk'

Hitchcock approaches the elevator and presses the control panel. He fastens the button on his jacket so it is tight against his naval. At the same time, a man identical to Hitchcock enters the lobby with a woman. As Max tries to comprehend two Hitchcocks, he sees two more patrol trucks pulling up outside.

Hitchcock steps into the elevator, waiting for Max. But Max looks at Hitchcock and then again looks back at the men outside. Two more Hitchcocks are approaching the entrance, each escorting a person. *Maybe more tournament qualifiers?*

The elevator rises up the sloping side of the building. Max examines the mechanisms and machinery left on display through the glass. Max thinks the levels between each floor look like the inside of a hollow glass coin. He spins to look behind him and over U City.

The elevator chimes as the doors slide apart diagonally on the eighth floor, and Hitchcock gestures for him to exit. Max steps cautiously out onto the glass floor. He can see everything below him, all the way to the bottom. Hundreds of souls are moving below him, keeping the APZON company and brand alive. Organisms within a vast organisation.

A boy of Max's age steps out of the other elevator across from him with another Hitchcock. He can see that the boy's hands have an odd red glow coming from under the skin.

Hitchcock clears his throat behind Max and gestures that he moves left. Max walks beside the boy and notices that he is visibly shaking. They are both followed by Hitchcocks. More Hitchcock-a-likes summon the elevators back to the lobby below. And more emerge from patrol trucks parked in the sandy parking lot outside.

As the sun starts to blaze outside, the inner building appears to tint and the glass walls and floors turn a smoky shade. The seventh floor smells pleasant; the air has a warm eucalyptus scent and the air feels refreshingly moist and cool.

The corridor forks at the end. The frightened boy is encouraged left with the indication of a single finger from the Hitchcock following him. Max turns right following the opposite instruction from his Hitchcock.

—

Max enters a busy room with everyone facing forward in rows of seats facing a large screen. Max sits quickly at the back. He figures it's smart not to stand out, to do what the crowd does. They vary in age and colour and gender.

Within moments, the screen at the front of the room blinks and flashes, and a loud voice reverberates around the room.

'Congratulations, qualifiers! You have reached the tournaments. You are deemed a citizen whose IQ is noteworthy. For this reason, you now have an opportunity to win a life of relaxation and blissful joy. But to get there, you will have to reach the eighth line and defeat the Cuboid Board! In doing so, you will gain followers and new branding. Please proceed to the next room to meet this week's pitching sponsors.'

Max has no idea what most of this means, but the crowd of people rise to their feet and swarm to a door under the screen. The boy he saw in the corridor remains seated in one of the rows, still staring at the screen, so Max moves up to sit beside him.

'You OK?' Max asks.

The boy looks away from the large screen for the first time. He seems startled by Max's presence and composes himself.

'Yeah. Yes, thank you. Just feeling a little lost. Alone. I suppose we're supposed to follow everyone.'

They both rise from among the empty chairs.

'But you aren't alone. I'm Max.'

'Conor,' he replies.

They follow the crowd through the door beneath the screen.

—

The small dimpled ball clangs against the window frame and ricochets back, a white blur that pings about the bachelor pad until there's the sound of smashing glass.

'Fucking sun.'

From the eighth floor, Skinner has a panorama of the world below. Everything is immaculate here; ordered, clinical, well-insulated from all that lies below. The walls that are not glass are filled with photos – a museum tour documenting the history of inventions from the last decade and the one before it. In front of an indented beanbag on the floor is a display wall of video game consoles. Even older machines are retrofitted so no cables are now required. Everything runs on Proximity Power Sourcing. But Skinner rubs his forehead. He glares with resentment out of the open side of the eighth floor at the yellow disc in the sky and thinks about the latest scores from the tournament. After all, he's a genius and never managed some of the scores he sees online.

'How do these kids get so fucking good?'

Wearing an open pink housecoat, shorts and odd furry slippers, he stands on a green mat beside the vast opening overlooking the city.

'I designed the fucking tournament,' he mutters to himself as he examines the head of the golf club.

'Sarah, another ball.'

The machine dutifully mounts another golf ball on a tee that appears from under the mat. Skinner swings again. This time, he doesn't slice the ball, and it goes spinning far outside into the sand.

'200 metres,' says a voice. 'A great shot.'

A chime of music fills Skinner's pad.

'You are placed 158. Good, but not quite good enough. Try again?'

Skinner's open pink housecoat spreads like a cape, and he spins 360 degrees before letting the golf club fly from his hand straight out the window.

He storms to his curved vending machine for a bottle of chilled water.

'Sir, is it not a good thing that the kids are so good at these things?' says Mole. 'They are future stock.'

Skinner takes a deep breath and appears to calm.

'Yes, of course, Mole. Thank you.'

But then he remembers the score he saw this morning and his face starts to redden. Suddenly he's yelling with fury.

'THINK YOU BEAT ME, #TIGERKILLER?

SOON YOU'LL NEED A JOB AND WHO WINS THEN, YOU LITTLE RUNT?

ADAM SKINNER DOES!'

Skinner's eye settles on the golf ball he embedded in a media screen on the wall earlier. Ripping it from its bracket, the large screen cracks in shards as he flings it to the glass floor. His slicked-back hair now flops about wildly in front of his eyes. Breathing heavily, Skinner replaces the fallen fringe to his scalp and slicks it back into place.

He glances at the broken pieces of the screen.

'Mole, get someone in here to clean that mess up,' he barks. 'And find #TigerKiller. Tell him he's won a prize and bring him here.'

Mole eyes him cautiously, standing well back in the corner of the room.

'Move! The longer I wait, the more I want something!'

Mole tucks his clipboard beneath his armpit and hurries away.

Skinner takes the control pad on his desk into his hand. It's time for a change. The building's glass instantly tints red. The entire building and everyone within it succumbs to the will of the man, Adam Skinner, APZON founder and CEO.

—

Alex keeps a slight distance from Winston. She questions herself and questions the other villagers' reactions. She would have avoided this whole mess if she listened to her father and stayed on her own side of the forest. Now her dad would know she disobeyed his instructions. Her priority is Max, but she decides to deal with one problem at a time. For now, she worries how others will react to Winston's presence. Bringing Max with her caused controversy, but a 70-year-old hunter who's armed? They are bound to be angry.

Winston hands Alex the rifle as they enter the mountain top village. Knots of people appear and stare; more streaming from their huts as word of the new arrival gets around.

Alex hooks the rifle strap over her shoulder as she leads through the middle of the huts. The murmuring of the villagers becomes louder, and she takes Winston's hand. Winston knows these people as 'the protesters'. The people of U City know them as 'the hippies' or lazy strikers. Alex regards them all as family and knows nothing but this way of life.

The curtain drops behind Alex's father as he exits his hut to investigate the growing din outside. As he takes in the scene, Sam conveys his displeasure to his daughter with a single dark look. He offers his hand to Alex, but she holds on to Winston's.

'Go with your father,' mutters Winston, trying to shake his hand free from hers and propel her to Sam's side.

Alex lets go of Winston's hand but stands between the two men.

'Dad, this is Max's grandad, and he needs our help.'

—

The auditorium hums with excited chatter. Max sees everyone milling around stalls and booths, their attention captivated by adverts, products and samples. Brand names are plastered on square kiosks and the frenzied people within pitch their products – clothing, shoes, accessories, tech-gadgets, jewellery, cosmetics, and even weapons. The brands vie to be associated with contestants who appear on the tournament channels; they pay a lot of money to be in the tournament pitch-room.

Max turns to look for Conor, but the boy has edged away from the everyone and walks through a door. Max senses danger from what lies behind that door, but a brand representative at the nearest table urgently beckons him.

'Me?' Max asks.

'Yes, you.'

'I've seen those shoes. Two? Three seasons ago?'

The sales rep leads Max to his stall.

'Now is your chance. A boy like you. What are you doing, wearing these?' he asks, tugging on Max's clothing. 'You're in luck, my boy. I have the perfect look. And let me be honest, you will be easy to improve.'

He waves a hand towards his wares.

'We are #StarQuality and we transform our clients to new highs. We raise everybody's influencing abilities with our clothing. Now what do you think of these?'

He hands Max a shoe.

'Do you prefer high fashion? Are you more street or dress wear? It is hard to tell with what you're wearing.'

The rep gathers a bundle of clothing in his arms as he ushers Max into the small booth. Max struggles to understand the whole concept.

'I already have shoes,' he says, pointing at his feet.

The man appears to have a bad taste in his mouth when he looks at the shoes.

'Heh-heh,' he chuckles. 'Yes, my boy. Very funny. You

are qualifier now and with it have the opportunities to wear the best and represent the best.'

'Really, I'm OK with these ones.'

'Boy, you are about to appear on billions of screens. Don't miss the opportunity to sell yourself!'

But Max shakes his head.

'My grandad just got these for me.'

'Listen,' the rep's attitude sharpens. 'If it's percentages you're wondering about, we have fantasy package rates for a kid like you. We can go as low as 70 per cent of all future earnings.'

He speaks too fast for Max to understand, and the crowd are gathering down further. Max moves to follow them.

'No, thank you.'

'Sixty-nine percent!'

The man walks with Max as he tries to leave.

'Sixty-eight?'

Then he's gone, as he spots a new opportunity.

You, sir! #StarQuality, you look like a man who seeks representation from the greatest brand in ...'

The screens around the room stop advertising and Skinner appears, the soles of his shoes visible as he reclines, feet up, behind his desk. He is dressed in a smart suit.

'This,' says Skinner, spreading a huge outstretched palm, in the lower corner of the screens, 'is the Arena floor.'

In one fluid movement, he pulls his feet from the desk and sits forward in his chair.

'This is where the greatest minds come to prove they are ready.'

He smiles into the zooming camera.

'Congratulations, you have been found to be the smartest minds in our society, and you will inevitably power the future.

'By now, you have selected your look and have signed with the brands you have chosen to represent.'

He rises from his desk to come right in front of the camera.

The door at the end of the room opens, and Max sees Hitchcocks – tens of them, larger than the ones he saw before – enter the room and circle around them. They each carry black batons with two rings circling the top.

Max looks up. Many Skinners appear to walk towards everyone in the room from multiple screens around the room.

'Now go! Get to your games. And ... ,' Skinner says, 'gooood luuuccckk!' On-screen Skinner finishes by sitting on his desk, arms crossed and then disappears. The flat screens resume advertising and a battery sold by APZON flashes up on the screen. A voice intones:

'There's a reason why our batteries have the impact they have on the world we live in. The unique combination of calcium, chloride, phosphorus, sodium, magnesium and potassium used in making the electrolyte inside our battery is our secret sauce; a secret sauce not used in other batteries.

Our secret electrolyte which has been globally patented was invented by APZON creator, owner and CEO, Mr Adam Skinner, just five years ago. And already its creation has impacted the globe on every level.

The electrolytes in our batteries cannot overheat, gift an eternal lifespan to the cells and mean an APZON battery never has to be charged.

So, no matter what industry you operate in, if you need to power your products, buildings, vehicles and more – use APZON batteries.
    APZON BATTERIES - Give your Products Life.'

One of the larger Hitchcocks approaches Max. The throng of guards close in on the qualifiers.

—

Inside the hut, Sam remains standing, and Winston feels his bristling hostility in the tight space. Alex hasn't stopped explaining and excusing since her dad lifted the blanket covering the door. She finally stops and looks at Winston.

'Sam? Can I call you Sam?' he asks.

He offers his hand in friendship and Sam accepts.

'You're doing a fantastic job raising this young lady. A task not easy in this environment, I know.'

When Sam inclines his head in acknowledgement, Winston relaxes. Somewhat.

'Alex tells me you knew my daughter.'

'She led our rebellion against Skinner and APZON.'

'Yes,' says Winston. 'She wrote about you with great respect and admiration in her letter. She was amazed at everyone's commitment to her. She knew everyone gave up so much to come here.'

'We gave up our old lives to come here and build a peaceful society. To see if it was even possible. We believed it was, and we thought we were achieving it.

But Sam shook his head.

'It turns out, we were tricked. As Sarah got closer to Adam Skinner, she got closer to the truth.'

Then Winston's words hit Sam.

'Letter? Sarah wrote you a letter ... how?'

'I have no idea,' says Winston, shrugging. 'Sarah and I had not spoken in over ten years. She stormed out of my home after an argument; I disapproved of her new boyfriend.'

'Adam Skinner?' Sam concludes.

Winston nods.

'The letter arrived at my house one morning in a filthy envelope. It was written over a year before I received it.'

'What did it say?' says Alex before Sam can.

'That I was right. That Adam was capable of terrible things and she had found out about experiments he was carrying out. She was worried what he'd do if he knew she wanted to leave him.

'She also told me where this place was, how to let her know when I got here (if I was coming). How to get in, where to wait for her when I was in.'

Winston remembers every word of that letter.

'She considered everything. She said she had evidence that she needed to get out; that the world needed to see what Skinner was really doing. She had our escape from here planned too, but she never got to tell me those details.'

Sam glances at Alex, and he thinks how he'd feel if he lost her.

Winston feels this is a good time to get to the point.

'Sam, my grandson is gone. Alex and I believe he's gone to U City to take part in a tournament – the chess games. 'Sarah told me to never let Adam get his hands on her baby. And that Skinner is capable of terrible things with the child.

'I've been keeping Max's existence a secret and keeping him hidden his whole life, and now ...'

'He's walked into the lion's den,' says Sam.

Grandad nods. Feeling a little less alone than he has felt for the past thirteen years.

'I'm...,'

'We're...,' Alex interjects

Winston starts again.

'We are going in to get him and could really do with numbers.'

Sam sits heavily on his bed suddenly feeling defeated. He looks up at Winston.

'I can't.'

His eyes wander about his home as he talks.

'I understand your position and support your actions as much as I supported your daughter's. But since we have been expelled from the city, I've been leading these people. This way of life has been a struggle to survive. Skinner is willing to kill to get what he wants; I've seen it, and I will not now lead my friends to their deaths.

'Your pursuit is noble, but my villagers are malnourished, and many are close to the end of their lives. They've been used as pawns in their lives already. I won't do it to them again.'

Sam gets to his feet again.

'There is a home here for you and Max if you make it back out. Get to him before he wins that tournament.'

Grandad nods and envelops Alex's father in a bear hug. His hand rests briefly on Sam's shoulder, and then he lifts the curtain-door and leaves.

Alex attempts to follow, but her father catches her hand and holds it tight.

He knows.

She knows.

'I'm proud of you,' he says, nodding approvingly. 'Be careful, and do not let him win that tournament.'

Alex hugs her father tight and follows after Grandad.

'Good luck,' whispers Sam after the curtain falls.

—

The jet of water falling down from above feels more refreshing than any swim Max has ever taken. When the water stops, he feels a breeze of warm drying air flowing from the same square shower sprinkler head above him. Max scratches his arm, and looks around the many white patches that are spreading about his body. He's dry when the air stops and the door opens. Max steps into a small room, and the wet door sucks closed behind him.

Prison-cell small, the room is white and furnished with a simple day-bed. The clothes he removed earlier remain on his bed. He gets dressed and waits, and finally the door opens again. Max goes to the door, and a woman darts down the hallway outside. Another person hurriedly passes his door and then two more people, running. Then many more. They all run in the same direction. No one spares even a glance in his direction.

Max holds on to the door frame as he watches the crowd. A thick black line runs down the centre of the corridor floor. The crowds, men, women, young and old, black and white, turn at the end of the corridor, following the black line.

Max steps out, and curiously follows in the same direction. But he stops as he feels the building vibrate beneath his feet. The place trembles and rumbles like an earthquake, then just as quickly as it began, the shaking stops. He continues, following the black line, the whole way along a corridor to the Arena – the tournament hall.

—

Skinner's knees bend to stabilise himself as his Citadel shakes in its frame.

'What was that?' he demands.

A boy cleaning up the broken screen freezes, hoping someone has an answer to his boss's question.

'Do you feel that? What the fuck is that?'

The boy sees Skinner is addressing a box on his aluminium desk and relaxes enough to continue cleaning.

'What is that?'

Chaotic noises of shouts, metal and smashing glass resound around Skinner's office over the intercom.

'Em, sir … ,' a voice can also be heard from the box.

'Em sir … what the fuck is it?'

'Sir, there's been a crash. Someone has crashed a strange vehicle through the front doors of the lobby.'

Skinner switches on a screen for the lobby. He can see a fire burn and rubble in the elevator lobby. Through the smoke he can see electrical sparks and a crumpled car. *Is that a Mustang?*

'The driver is a man…,' the guard says, 'with something wrong with his skin.'

Skinner shakes his head in frustration.

'Something wrong with his skin?'

He questions the intelligence of the people born in his city.

'Is he old?'

'Ah, yes sir, Mr Skinner, sir. Maybe.'

'Get rid of him.'

Skinner releases the intercom button and circles his desk to adjust the freshly hung new screen with his fingers and thumbs.

'Sir,' the voice over the intercom continues hesitantly, 'he says he is Sarah's father.'

Skinner freezes for an instant. He shoos the staff like a frantic mime artist – not making a sound. When he's the only one left in the office, he depresses the intercom button again.

'Bring Mr Turk to the eighth floor. My office.'

—

Rounding the corner, the corridor opens suddenly onto a massive open space. The eighth floor Arena hall has no ceiling. A viewing platform runs around the walls up at the height the ninth floor should be. The room continues to disappear up to the inner cone within the roof of the Citadel. Lights, screens, score-numbers are suspended from the inverted cone above. The siren, also dangling from the cone, sounds a loud buzzing blast, causing Max to jump and people to rush chaotically towards tables around the Arena floor. The seats are filled in seconds, and every chair is occupied – except for one in the first row right beside him.

The room seems to vibrate with excitement. The buzzer from the siren sounds a second time, and a blue glow lights up one side of Max's face. With near military precision, the sound levels drop in the Arena and the mass dance of game play begins.

Amid the hum of activity, Max hears the clicks of moving pieces touching the boards and the clacks of chess clock buttons being hit by palms. He watches the contestants' glowing hands and 63 games of chess being played, side by side, row by row.

—

Skinner scurries about his office, tidying surfaces, ensuring everything is in its place. The far wall slides, slowly revealing a window onto the Arena floor. His office is an observation deck and from behind mirrored glass, he's perfectly positioned to oversee the tournament streaming live throughout U City. Skinner only notices the tournament has begun as the light of the Arena hits his office.

'Fuck, not now! I don't have time for this.'

'Sir, you said to never stop the tournament schedule? Should I stop? ...'

The clipboard quivers as Mole utters the words.

'No!' Skinner yells. Shoving several items into his desk drawer, he makes eye contact with the assistant.

'I didn't say stop the tournament. There must be no gaps in the production line.'

Skinner removes the pink housecoat and flings it over Mole. He slides back a locker door to survey a row of suits. Skinner turns to the glass where he sees his ghostly reflection before the tournament floor. He hangs a suit from below his neck before rejecting it. Taking another suit he does it again. This time keeping a hold of the suit, he slides the door shut.

'Is he on his way up? How near is he?'

Mole watches a blue and red dot rising through a 3D rendition of the building displayed on his digi-clipboard.

'Sir, the driver of the vehicle is in the elevator with 39 as we speak.'

'Fuck, nearly here,' Skinner squeaks as he hops on one foot pulling on a shoe. 'Get the fuck out.'

As the man turns, Skinner pulls a shoe onto the other foot, but then he notices something behind Mole's clipboard.

'What is that?'

The man stops and turns around, worried.

'Sir?'

'That,' Skinner says, pointing at the clipboard and advancing upon it.

'That,' he says, pulling the journal the man has tucked behind the clipboard.

'Where did you get this?'

Skinner runs his hand across the name – Dr Sarah Turk.

'Si ... sir ...'

'Si ... si ... si ... Well?'

'Sir, it was found on one of this tournament's qualifiers. It's an APZON research journal, so I told the guard I'd take a look at it,' Mole replies with a quiver.

Skinner heads straight for the window overseeing the Arena.

'One of those had this? Which one?'

'Ah, sir, the guard did not take note which participant he took the paper from.'

'Why the fuck not?' Skinner growls.

He stares at the Arena floor outside, examining the faces at the tables.

'Tell me Mole, would anyone be able to identify the child? Differentiate it from any normal child, if we have it in our possession for ... examination?'

'The child, sir?'

The slender man struggles to follow.

'Yes the child. The original child. The one we put into Dr Turk.'

The man's eyes dart around as he desperately tries to remember.

'You ... hired me and the doctors to make it undetectable. To make them undetectable. And now I do not know if we could ever know with certainty if ...'

The man physically shrinks as he continues.

'I did my job.'

Skinner's face snarls in the window's reflection, and he clenches a fist.

'Fuuuccking ...'

His face relaxes quickly.

' ... marvellous.'

As he strides across the room to Mole, he removes a pen from the inside pocket of his jacket. Mole doesn't even have time to react as Skinners fist drives the pen into his assistant's eardrum. His closed fist remains against Mole's head for a moment, and the aide's face remains frozen. Skinner releases his grip on the pen, and the man drops onto the ground. He kicks the desk chair with force, sending it flying across the glass floor of the office to hit the Arena window.

—

It takes two guards to lift Grandad from the seat of the Mustang. The old man appears dazed and unable to get to his feet. A third guard stands between the steel and glass debris and the Mustang, receiving instruction from his radio.

'Mr Skinner says bring him up to the eighth floor,' he says as the two others try to prop the old man against the car.

'Crazy old bastard,' one of them grunts as they haul him towards the elevator.

Winston flutters an eyelid and sneaks a peek of his surroundings. He sees the elevator door close.

The third guard remains in the lobby, monitoring the hole Grandad has made in the building's ground floor. The boot of the Mustang lifts slowly behind him amid falling debris and showers of sparks. Just as he turns, Nat, Thackeray and Alex rain down on him, wrestling him into silence. Hitchcock 42 wonders how he'll explain this as the boot of the Mustang closes over his head.

Nat helps Thackeray carry their bag to the elevator door. Inside, Thackeray holds the elevator door, anxiously waiting for Alex. He can see her legs as she leans into the back seat of the Mustang. She emerges rifle in hand. She stops only to rummage in the rubble on the lobby floor to fish out the guard's dropped radio.

'I heard them say the eighth floor.'

Thackeray presses the button for the eighth floor. Nat attributes his breathlessness to a combination of adrenaline and the weight of the bag on his back.

'Do you think that's where they brought Max too? Eighth?'

As they reach the fifth floor the radio in Alex's hand speaks.

'Guard down. In the lobby ...'

She stops the elevator and the three lean closer, listening carefully to the two-way.

'We have suspicious activity down here.'

They wait until the voice instructs another.

'Search the building ...'

They know they are already running out of time.

—

Max goes to the empty chair and the only game which has not started on time. Nobody pays him any attention, not even the guards dispersed around the outer wall. Max only sees impatience on the brow of the woman facing him. She stares through Max and then at the clock on the table. Max moves a pawn one square forward then presses the timer clock under the woman's watchful eyes. She moves her first piece, and just as quick, presses the timer clock with her glowing red hand.

Max looks at the hand and the red light somehow coming from inside it. He looks around the Arena floor. Other hands he can see also glow with a faint red from underneath the skin of their right hands.

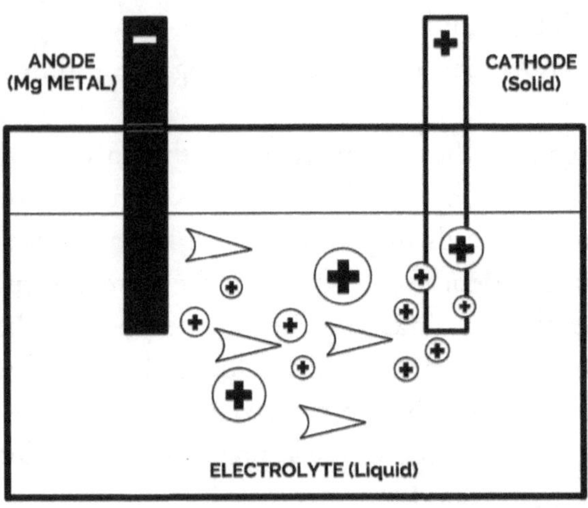

ANODE
(Mg METAL)
CATHODE
(Solid)
ELECTROLYTE (Liquid)

Chapter 9

The Factory Line

The sudden squealing of chair legs alerts him to another game ending two minutes later and then another, minutes after that. Games are finishing all over the Arena floor. Players bow and the winners move to their next row to await their next opponent.

Max hears the clock tick inside his head. He has been lining up a back-rank mate and now notices a mate in two. His opponent does not see it, or at least is not defending against it. Max checkmates the game, and the woman springs up in front of him like a Jack-in-the-box. She bows, and Max watches her walk away without a word. He sees her follow a white glowing line all the way down the Arena until she disappears through a door.

He realises a light is flashing under his own feet, leading in the opposite direction. He follows an L-shaped trail to another table and a waiting man. His opponent is a big man, probably six feet tall when standing, with dark brown skin and hair in snake coils like Alex's and a glowing hand. The man smiles at him. He is a good chess player, better than the last, but he still needs practise. Légall mate is beyond his knowledge, and Max proceeds on the grid with relative ease.

—

Skinner ties his long hair back from his face. When a loose, shorter section of fringe falls and swings in front of his eyes, he palms it back, so it sits sleek and oiled on his head.

He shrugs to fix his jacket cuffs and adjusts his tie in the reflection of the glass. He pulls in a deep breath and exhales slowly and calmly. He glances irritably at his assistant slumped the floor, blood pooling and thickening around his head.

His forehead furrows as he leans closer to his reflection in the window. He reassures himself that he looks intimidating. He drops into the chair and raises his feet, crossing his ankles on his desk.

'Ok, bring him in now,' he announces into the intercom.

As the door clicks, he uncrosses his ankles and lets his legs fall to the floor. Fidgety, he chooses to stand.

As Winston enters between two guards, he sees Skinner's hands shoved into his suit trouser pockets and his shoulders near touching his ears. He also spots the assistant's body slumped in blood in the corner.

'He came quietly?' Skinner asks the guards.

But Winston disregards everyone in the room and moves straight to the Arena window.

The guards stand uneasy, unsure of what they should do.

Winston spots Max in the row furthest from the window, and almost winces in pain with the relief of seeing him again.

'Our tournament floor is impressive, isn't it?' says Skinner.

Winston turns around.

'You can leave us,' Skinner says, addressing the guards. 'But stay close outside the door.' Winston is reminded of the cowardly lion in the story. He's distracted by the guards leaving and doesn't see Skinner slide a letter-opener on his desk into the back of his waistband.

When the guards leave, Winston looks at Skinner for the first time. Not in the eye, because Skinner is carefully avoiding his gaze. He sees the part of Skinner that the respected trillionaire has managed to hide from so many. The old man can see it, and Skinner knows it.

—

The elevator door opens on the fifth floor. Alex sticks her foot in the door to keep it from closing.

'We need to find the stairs,' she says scanning the hall.

'…permission to shoot,' adds the disembodied voice on the radio.

Nat also pokes his head into the empty hallway.

The three file out; staying close to the wall and moving at speed towards the end of the corridor.

A woman in a skirt rounds the corner ahead of them coming straight for them. The three stop with fright. Her head is down as she scrolls through a tablet in her hands. She looks up as she passes between the three, but her glance is brief and disinterested. Her head is quickly down again into her screen as she hurries on.

Alex, Nat and Thackeray breathe again and scurry around the same corner where the woman came. The skirted lady stops and takes a second to look back. She looks into the empty corridor and returns to scrolling and strolling. However, she hears the sounds of footsteps and looks back to see the three youths returning in her direction at speed. Alex cradles the rifle in her arms as she keeps pace with Thackeray and Nat is right behind them. They pass the skirted woman like whirlwinds as four guards chase round the corner with guns aloft.

'Get down!' roars a uniformed pursuer in front.

The skirt-wearing woman hits the floor of the corridor. The guard watches through the scope just as Nat turns the corner. Too late to shoot, the guards continue the chase.

—

They sprint through the marketing department's office floor, a room filled with cubicles. Men and woman yelp in frightened confusion as the armed guards dart pass their short-walled work cells.

'Get down!' a guard yells again as they follow the trio's route through the grey room.

Nat pushes through double doors at the end. The three face stairwells in two directions: two ways up and two ways down.

'Split up!' Alex cries. 'No matter what happens, see you two at the top.'

'We do this together,' says Nat.

Alex steps in closer.

'We are doing this together,' she says. She hands him the rifle and points behind hm at the other stairwell.

'I'll see you both on the roof.'

Then she kisses him and runs up the stairwell behind her, leaving Nat with an empty rifle and some hope.

Nathaniel lies the rifle on the steps. He kicks the butt, splitting the wood in half.

Nat jams one half through the handles of the double doors before they start for the roof.

'You remember there are no bullets, right?' Thackeray says. He wonders why Nat is bothering to carry the rifle at all.

The first guard to reach the double doors hits it hard with his face. The doors refuse to budge. His face meets the doors a second time as a colleague lands on top of him, pushing him hard from behind.

Four guards push together, trying to force the doors. Others begin back through the office for an alternate route to pursue the intruders.

—

Max wonders about the large, red button on the edge of his sixth-row table. This red button is new. Eyeing the Lucena position in two moves, Max waits for the endgame. That's when he learns what the red button is all about. His opponent slams the button with his palm, and the board lifts an inch off the table and rotates 180 degrees from its original placing.

Max finds himself sitting now at the white side of the board with his new king in trouble and two moves from check. The almost endless numbers of moves within the game of chess dance with a thumping beat in Max's mind. Then, suddenly, it's as if the room, the building, the whole city and world falls away. He feels the stars surrounding him as he sits with the table, the board and the pieces. The possibilities appear, kaleidoscopic and swirling, in his mind's eye. He listens to the patterns, numbers flying by him, his chair in the centre of the blackness of space. Max is pinned to his seat as the room spins and twists as in a gyroscope, smooth and free. He travels upside down, sideways with yawing motions, moving and turning with speed. The chess pieces move with him, staying on the board as he remains fixed in the chair somehow. He wonders whether to move the pieces or the stars.

Max's surroundings return from star-filled space to the Arena. He tries to think of practicalities. If the red button flips the board, can it flip it back? If so, how many times can it be used? How many in total, and how many for each player?

But he feels the patterns, and now his hands paint them with the chess pieces. The patterns dance before Max eyes. As he moves each piece, he eyes a woman approach, waiting to occupy the loser's chair.

In six moves, Max fights his white pieces back to an advantageous position on the board and sets up two possible checks, one at either end of the board: mirrored Lucena positions. His opponent moves exactly how Max expects until he checks Max's king. Checkmate.

However, checkmate is only checkmate if you cannot get out of it. And it is Max's turn to play; he slams the button. The board spins to checkmate his opponent. But now it's his opponent's move. Max has gambled and wonders if it has worked. The man across the table uses this turn to press the button, desperation written across his face. The board does not spin. Game over, and Max bows and proceeds to the next row having learnt that it's one spin each on row six.

He has figured out a new set of rules on row six of the Arena. He must anticipate new surprises and new capabilities in this new row. The game he is far from perfecting is expanding in difficulty. He realises he has no idea of the challenges ahead.

—

'How is Sarah?' says Skinner, idly tracing a finger across his desk.

'My daughter is dead.'

The old man's voice is cold and dry.

Skinner sits back into his chair, his weight wheeling it back from the table.

'Oh,' he says, staring at a point where the floor meets the wall.

Winston turns his back to Skinner again to watch Max from the distance. His eye connects with his reflection staring back at him in the window.

'All this time,' says Skinner, 'I thought she had just not come back. I thought she had changed her mind. Left me here.'

Skinner stands, his hands shoved into his pants pockets.

'How?' he says, watching the old man for any movement. 'When?'

Winston feels that old tide of pain rise behind the skin of his face. Forced to think about that day again, he once again wishes his daughter never met Skinner. He should have never introduced them. He swallows hard, and his eyes blink. The smell of the dead man's blood fills his nostrils.

Skinner approaches. He places a hand on Winston's shoulder. The old man's head turns to icily stare at the hand, and Skinner yanks it away as though the shoulder is too hot to touch.

'She died in the birth.'

Skinner steps closer to the Arena window. In his mind, he sees an explosion of present, future and past.

The implantation had taken. Hadn't it? Child birth, the old man says. Perhaps it was a success. Did the child survive? Why is the old man now here? But Sarah..? No.

Skinner needs to fill the silence.

'Nobody has to die anymore. You see?'

Winston glances at the dead assistant heaped so disrespectfully on the floor.

Skinner becomes defensive.

'We're doing good things here. I have enough data on Sarah to code her a million times over. The greater good requires smaller sacrifices.'

'You can talk to her again,' he smiles. 'And I, super-genius and trillionaire extraordinaire, have cured the aging process.'

He spreads his arms wide.

'Can you imagine how much money we'll make?'

Winston looks Skinner in the eyes, which the latter interprets as interest.

'Come, let me show you a tour,' he says, proudly holding open the door to the hallway.

Winston crouches by the corpse on the floor and shuts the man's eyes. He crosses himself and makes the sign of the cross over the body in prayerful respect.

Skinner's colour rises. He burns inside at this display of religious cultism at the epicentre and peak of his creation. *Smuggled poison*, he thinks. Skinner uses the hallway to calm down. Meanwhile, Winston gently removes the pen from the assistant's ear and slides it into his pocket before following Skinner outside.

—

Alex climbs two floors with speed. Something catches her eye through a small glass panel on the door of that floor. On her toes, she peeks through the window. She sees the sign, Level 7. It looks quiet, empty and safe, and slowly she exits and lets the door close again behind her. She finds herself in a large, white open room. Fluorescent bulbs light up the floor space, shining out from underneath four island countertops.

It looks like a laboratory of sorts, a messy one. The island counters are littered with wires, plants, plants in jars, empty jars, bell jars, seeds and things Alex can't identify. A spliced plant grows between two panes of glass, roots and foliage exposed. Upon closer inspection, Alex sees it has wires growing from it instead of real roots.

She freezes as she hears a sudden scratching noise. It's soft and distant, but she hears it nonetheless. She struggles to locate it exactly. Peering towards the dark, back end of the room, she sees a grid of transparent rectangular boxes. The noise appears to come from back there.

Moving closer, she notes another door, slightly ajar, but she passes it. It's darker down this end of the room where the white becomes grey. But she isn't brave enough to look for a light for fear it draws attention to her. She is determined to find the source of the curious scratching before she leaves. She leaps as a blood-spattered pigeon slams against the wall of the transparent acrylic box directly in front of her face. It screeches, scurries and scratches, thumping against all four of its walls.

Alex moves down along the rows of boxes covering the wall. There are pigeons in each of the acrylic boxes, some scratching at the clear walls. Some are hiding beneath bedding, and other pigeons lie motionless. Alex has lived her life in a place where the only living things are people. These unusual creatures puzzle her greatly.

She sees a featherless creature with blue skin. Another is turning in a circle, standing at the centre of the box turning, turning, turning. Alex wonders if the pigeon has started this little twirling dance for her benefit? If not, how long has the strange creature been turning? And why?

She hears another sound. A tapping. She follows it to the far end of the row of acrylic boxes. At that end, many of the pigeons are lifeless. Some are certainly dead, but the tapping continues.

—

Again, Max notes that reddish light under the skin of his opponents' hands. The opponents change, but the lights within their hands do not. He scratches his own hand where the white patches first appeared. He is often scratching there, he realises.

An opponent sits opposite Max, and he looks over to face Conor. Placing his hand on the table opposite Conor's, Max looks at his own hands. His initial curiosity over the light in his opponents' hands becomes a painful, flashing memory. But it's vague, more a feeling than a memory. Max struggles to recall it. Max's hand, where his opponent's chips are located, is now a patchwork of brown and white pigment; as if his colour is flaking.

Conor follows Max's eyes and briefly stares at Max's scarred hand. The two boys lock eyes, and Max wonders why Conor is tapping on the table. The siren sounds and the commotion of gameplay begins. The clocks start ticking. Max's opponent taps his finger by the board again.

Conor opens the game and opens well. Max recognises it in parts. It might be a combination of known and complementing openings in one. Max admires it, but quickly finds himself in trouble.

—

As they walk along the hallway, Winston clears his throat.

'You won't build, code or create any form of artificial abomination of my daughter. I won't let that happen.'

Skinner, already fired up inside, feels his hands clench with rage in his pockets. He only pulls out a hand so the elevator can scan his thumb.

'Death is what makes us alive,' says Winston. 'The best gift in life is that it ends. Because it's limited, it has value.'

They both avoid eye contact when they step inside.

'I won't let you take that value away, Adam.'

'How do you intend stopping me?' Skinner snarls as the diagonal elevator doors close.

He turns to glare at Winston, and the sneer on his face disappears.

—

The tapping becomes a thudding noise as she gets closer. It is coming from inside one of the boxes – at the far end of the room. Alex finally finds the source. In one of the last boxes, one of these feathered creatures is running itself headfirst into the glass.

It's repeated butting has splashed the transparent surroundings of its cage with blood. As she stands there watching, more and more blood pours from the seeping, butting head. Alex looks away disturbed by the sight. Then she is startled by the sight of the most unusual pigeon of all. In a box below the thumping, bloodied pigeon, is a sight that bewilders her. The pigeon is physically shaped like the others, but instead of feathers or bare skin, this creature has organic leaves growing through its hair follicles. Real plant leaves.

She blinks before leaning closer in awe. Moving her head from side to side, she checks for possible tricks in the reflection of the glass. But a loud noise comes from beyond the ajar door behind her. She moves to the door. *Could it be? Is that Max's voice?* Pushing the door back the remains of the way with her fingertips, she holds her breath.

What she sees is even more unexpected than the leafy pigeon. She spots a bodyless forearm mounted on the table and pointing up at the ceiling. It appears to be a full human arm. She steps closer to survey the entire table. She sees hands, fingers, a jar of eyes, skinless mechanical faces, robotic limbs, a jar of hair and ... more eyes, each on top of tiny pillars like they are sitting on golf tees or slim egg cups. She leans closer to the eyeballs, scanning each of them, moving down the row. One of the eyeballs blinks.

Alex stumbles, knocking the table behind and toppling the forearm. She manages to catch it before it hits the ground. Replacing the forearm carefully, she turns to find the eyes have rolled off their pillars. She sees an eyeball roll off the edge of the table and run across the floor.

Without thinking much, Alex chases it down the room, head down, until the eyeball stops at a person's foot. The feet are bare and they do not moved as the eye rests against it. Terrified, Alex steps back, straightens her back and looks into the face.

Looks into his face.

Max's face.

—

Max's opponent taps his finger on the table. *Tap-tap, tap-tap-tap, tap-tap, tap-tap-tap.*

Max tries to concentrate. He wonders if Conor is trying to distract him. He thinks it may be working.

Tap-tap, tap-tap-tap, tap-tap, tap-tap-tap.

Still bloody tapping. But Max concentrates and adopts a zen state of acceptance. He plays well and holds more pieces. Maybe the tapping has a benefit. Could it be therapeutic? It is constant, and it has rhythm.

Tap-tap, tap-tap-tap, tap-tap, tap-tap-tap.

It does have a rhythm.

Tap-tap, tap-tap-tap, tap-tap, tap-tap-tap.

It's two taps, three taps, then two taps again. It just stops and starts over again. He's sure of it. It's Morse code. Dots and dashes. Or taps?

Tap-tap, tap-tap-tap, tap-tap, tap-tap-tap.

It's just like the code from the bunker. Can he remember it? Having only seen it once for a short time, Max is unsure. He stills himself. Then listens to his head. The letters and the code chart appear for him to see. He spells out the boy's message.

S ... O ... S.

—

It is Max's face, but it has no eyes. It, he, whatever it is, does not have eyes. Alex sees darkness in the sockets where eyes should be. Eyes are the windows to the soul, and there are no eyeballs.

Alex looks into Max's face, or rather a face like his. The skin on the face and naked torso looks like real skin. It might even be real she thinks as her hand reaches out to touch it. It feels like skin as she slides her hand along the torso to the where the heart would be.

'Don't move!' says a voice from behind her.

Alex jumps, pulling her hand back and spinning around onto her toes.

'Freeze!'

Alex hears the voice but sees no one behind her.

'Don't move, freeze, freeze, cold, need a sweater, don't get cold, cold-freeze. Damn it! Back where I started ...'

The words are nonsensical, rambling and come from low behind one of the island desks beside her. Alex stretches on to her toes to peer over the counter top. The floor beyond it is littered with papers, folders, a smashed laptop and monitor screens. She walks around the desk and spots someone's leg sticking out from under the pile. This leg is clad in long pants and has shoes. Women's shoes.

'Hello?' says Alex. 'Are you ok?'

The voice responds.

'Hello, are you ok? Are you ok? Hello. Ok ... hell ... ooooo.'

Alex steps carefully into the pile of items. The pile shifts under her feet and she reaches down for a broken laptop. Picking up the smashed device, she finds a face underneath, looking back at her.

'Hello. Ok. Freeze. Sweater ...'

'Why do you keep repeating things?' says Alex as she uncovers the woman buried under piles of paper files.

'Who are you? You shouldn't be here,' the woman protests. 'You didn't touch anything, did you? Or anything didn't touch you for that matter? Matter? Yes, matter. All matter. Every matter. It is, in fact, all matter. But does it matter?'

Alex helps the woman to her feet. Once upright, the woman dusts down her white lab coat and stands with her hands placed on her hips in a superhero pose. Her strawberry blonde hair is cut in an erratic, choppy manner. She's very tall, six feet three or four. She is unusual looking but beautiful in Alex's eyes.

'You didn't touch anything, did you?' the woman says looking around.

'I tried not to. Are you ok? Why are you lying under a pile of ... stuff? And in the dark?'

Alex has so many questions.

'Oh, you know ... ,' the woman says, still looking around, 'how Monday's are. Ha-ha.'

What a weird woman. What a weird place, Alex thinks, her eyes drawn again to the Max doppelgänger.

'That? Do you like that?' the woman asks. 'I made it. Him. I made him. I made all of them. Bio-tech-A.I crosses.'

The woman approaches the Max-like figure.

'Yes, good, but not perfect. I'm having trouble with emotions particularly.'

'Who isn't, lady?' mutters Alex.

'I think I came close once. I am most certain of it, but ...'

The woman places her hands back on her hips and sighs as she gazes at Max's look-alike.

'Unfortunately, that specimen disappeared. Well, it was stolen many years ago, and I had to start all over again. I lost a lot of data. All very exciting stuff. Break-ins, break-outs, ha-ha!'

She never seems to laugh but instead makes a 'ha-ha' sound as if to let Alex know she can identify 'funny'.

'But he's gone nonetheless. Perhaps the perfect specimen. One of a kind. Gone.'

The scientist lady continues to make exaggerated shapes with her lips for long after she finishes speaking.

'When?' Alex asks.

'Oh, I don't know. It's hard to keep track of time in here – APZON and The Squares.'

A picture hangs crookedly on the wall near Alex. She examines it. It appears to be an architectural diagram – three structural squares containing square compounds evenly spaced out. The rambling woman looks at it too but only to watch her own reflection on the glass within the frame.

'Years ago.'

Touching her face in the reflection. 'Ten? Fifteen? Maybe.'

'That's my friend,' Alex says as she reaches out to touch the inanimate version of Max again.

The woman laughs.

'Oh no, that one isn't even on. Alive? Cognitive?'

She searches for the word.

'Ha. And people come in here and say I'm mad.'

Alex cuts through the woman's joviality with a sharp tone in her voice.

'Not that one. The one from years ago. That thing looks just like my friend. Just like him but Max is alive.'

Alex remembers why she is in the Citadel.

'Max is real. He's loving, caring, soft in every way, but he's strong too. He's smart. Because he doesn't care what people think of him. He's never afraid or ashamed to ask a question. He cares more for the knowledge than what someone might think of him. He has shown me the meaning of true humanity. He's why I came here.'

Alex heads for the door. She has to find the real Max.

'No, he's not here,' the woman says, following Alex. 'I looked. Well, I didn't look but the guards, they looked. They searched the whole building and the whole compound.

He never left the perimeter, but he's definitely not in this building. Somewhere possibly – but not here. That specimen was lost years ago.'

Alex has a fierce light in her eye as she turns back to address the woman.

'He is not a specimen! He's a person. He looks just like that thing, but he's my friend. And he's 13.'

The woman looks animated and excited.

'He cannot be like these,' she says.

She darts to the paper-pile from which buried her and begins to rummage through wads of bound papers. She finds what she is looking for.

Alex sees the journal the woman opens is identical to the ones belonging to Max's mam. But when the strange woman shines a blue light on the empty pages inside, they fill with diagrams and photographs. They are hiding in the pages of the journal.

'Look, these are not real humans,' she says. She flicks on a desk lamp and opens the journal under it. 'They're nana-tech-biological blends. They are born and raised just like an ordinary person, but their origin is half-human.'

The woman checks for comprehension in Alex's face.

'They are female human eggs impregnated with nana-tech. Half A.I and half biological. Humanity will always be a choice. We've had problems getting the specimens to choose their human sides.'

Alex remembers the bunker.

'They aren't blank – the journals. Where did the female eggs come from? Max's mam worked here years ago. So, maybe, Max was the original.'

Alex searches the woman's eyes.
'The eggs were Max's mother's? So Max is…'

Chapter 10

Decoding the Truth

Nat leads Alex, Winston, Thackeray through the trees to the bunker. Nat's feet land by Alex, but his attention is totally absorbed by the Mustang. Winston lifts the bonnet, and Nat's disbelief turns to excitement as the old man explains the workings.

With a heave of a rope, the board covering the chamber shifts back even further. Winston knows the opening is enough to bring the Mustang up. Time is limited. Max needs their help. Thackeray and Winston begin to work overground, lowering a rope to Nat and Alex. Alex eyes are on the lantern flame in the bunker, but she helps Nat lace the rope through the car grill – back and forth to one another.

'OK, let's do this,' says Nat standing again.

Raising his voice, he shouts back up above.

'OK, we've tied this end.'

'On three, you push, we pull,' Winston replies. 'Alex, you get in and steer.'

Alex extinguishes the lantern, missing the warmth of the flame and the comfort it gives. When her eyes adjust, she notices the smoke-trail bend as if following a draught. *What is this?* she thinks. *How can there be a draught in the lower depths of a underground bunker?* Yet the pages on the top of the journals flicker. There's a breeze somewhere, whistling. She looks around the shelves and feels it, escaping from behind the wall.

She flicks through the stack of writing journals, but the pages are blank.

—

Skinner sees Winston's forbidding expression, but he continues as the elevator rises.

'Maybe you don't want to speak to her because you're afraid. You're afraid of what she might have to say. Afraid what she ...'

The old man raises a finger, stopping him.

The elevator doors open, and Skinner scurries out ahead. He turns with his hands spread, looking back at the old man, inviting him to behold everything around him. Winston cannot avoid seeing the cruciform shape of Skinner's silhouette against the light behind him.

He follows, stepping out of the elevator onto a steel platform after Skinner. The ninth floor is a steel-ringed viewing platform that only Skinner's fingerprint can access. Winston glances over the railing to the tournament floor below, and up at the cone-shaped siren and scoreboard overhead on the tenth floor. On the rafters above, he spots Alex and begins to count in his head.

'You cannot play God, Adam,' Winston says.

Skinner cannot hold it anymore. The fire within him explodes, and he reddens to near purple in fury. The trillionaire aims the heel of an expensive shoe into the old man's mid-section, forcing Winston back against the railings. Winston tries to scramble back to his feet, but Skinner's boot and body weight presses upon him.

'I can forgive you coming out here to save your daughter,' Skinner hisses. 'I might even forgive you keeping the child from me this whole time. But this ...'

Skinner reaches behind him and pulls out the journal taken from Max, tucked between his belt and back.

'To Kill a Mockingbird, Alice in Wonderland,' Skinner says out as he flicks through the pages. 'And how fitting – Frankenstein. That was her favourite. Bastardised pieces of literature.'

Skinner rips pages out and rolls them into a ball which he throws at Winston in disgust.

'Now I know you're fond of a good bastard. You've raised one. And if I remember correctly, Sarah told me you are one.'

He strides along the platform, laughing as he continues to shred the pages.

'But what use is fiction? Made up. Not a trace of science. Fairy-tale and art; rust to sciences' steel.'

He lets the torn pages flitter from his hands. Winston lets Skinner ramble in his fury and crawls back into the elevator. *The time is close now,* he thinks. The ripping stops as Skinner reaches the final few pages between the cover. He advances on Winston, holding the cover back, and presenting the back page in the old man's own writing.

–

'We have a problem with that speci ...'

The white-coated woman is stopped in her tracks by Alex's malign look.

' ... boy. We have a problem with that boy. That's why we haven't gone into production. Intelligence. It has been made clear to me that I have achieved too much in that area. I have done my job too well. Ha-ha.'

'What?'

Alex is bewildered.

'They ... sorry, he is too intelligent. Capable of out-thinking myself, Mr Skinner, even the computational predictions of all our software.'

Alex smiles at this.

'That's why Mr Skinner has introduced the chess tournament. Research suggests that such a tournament would net the top intellectuals in the wider population. Thus giving Mr Skinner a way to identify the outliers with ... troublesome levels of intelligence.'

'Troublesome?'

The woman's head and limbs look jerky, jittery, over-excited, but she becomes still before she answers.

'You don't know what happens to the winners of this tournament, do you?'

—

Max looks up from the board and into the boy's eyes. The boy looks back into his – relieved. One of the guards, standing against the outer wall, watches suspiciously, as the two boys' eyes meet in understanding.

The boy begins to tap again, and Max notes the letters behind his eyes as his fingers send a message: D.O.N.T ... W.I.N ...

'I wandered off but was brought back,' says Conor. 'Not before I found a room in this building. I don't know what it's for, but it's hot and smells of rot.'

His eyes dart towards a door over Max's shoulder. Conor is looking towards a room where Max saw a winner entering earlier.

'A terrible smell,' the boy says with a shudder.

Max knows the smell he talks of. He smelled it in the air by the lake; the smell fills the pump-houses and waters the trees. The same smell falls from the dust clouds that float over the forest. Then he sees the guard making his way towards their table.

—

Alex stops for breath on the stairs and notices splashes of yellow paint on the steps. The ceiling has recently been painted. She yanks a lever and the bell-housing of the fire alarm on the wall begins to vibrate in the stairwell. A loud buzzing fills the air and Alex looks down to see the steps below her fill with APZON staff evacuating the building..

'What was that?'

Alex hears the radio speak again.

'It's the fire alarm, sir.'

'Well? Is there a fire?'

'Sensors don't show a fire, sir. The alarm has been tripped on the eighth floor and ...'

'It's a false alarm. The old man hasn't come alone. Not a single guard leaves this building. Do you hear me? And the tournament continues. I have customers to please, numbers to meet.'

Skinner's concentration returns to his immediate surroundings.

'Let me finish up here, and I'll be right down.'

—

Skinner follows Winston into the elevator and presses a button before turning his attention to Winston once again.

'It's this I cannot forgive,' he said as he rips the last page of the journal containing the Ten Commandments.

'The original battle – religion versus science. They have been at war like black and white for years. I have built a society for the greater good, based solely on science. And now I find you've brought this here.'

Winston spits blood and touches his lip. He smiles with blood-smeared teeth as he straightens up after the surprise blow.

'I'm not even that religious,' the old man laughs, fuelling more of Skinner's hatred. 'The stories are the best versions I can remember. It's not easy transcribing books from memory. But I think I get the lessons across.'

Winston considers the time it has taken him to put the memories to paper.

'You didn't make it easy for me,' he says. 'There's not a single work of fiction in this whole place.'

Winston exhales, feeling tired.

'You can't build a perfect society without art, without wonder and dreams and imagination. We need minds crazy enough to think of flying ships, computers and reaching for planets for scientists to have goals. Artists paint the dreams; scientists take us to them. We progress together, two pairs of feet walking. Religion is like art – designed to provoke thought within one's self. And science is the same – our attempt to understand existence and our place in it.'

Winston knows it must be near the time now, so he finishes.

'Religion, art and science evolve as times change. I have not brought religion here. You have. The only thing needed to motivate good people to align is the presence of evil.'

—

Whether the science-driven caveman stepped outside the cave to prove the storyteller among them was right or wrong is irrelevant. Art motivates us to seek truth. - The Author

—

When the radio chatter stops, Alex continues sprinting up the steps. She ascends the steps as Skinner and Winston descend in the elevator. She climbs until there are no more stairs, and she pushes a door and stumbles out on the ninth-floor platform.

She hangs over the balcony to see rows, columns, tables and players with their heads down. Her eyes scan the tournament floor grid, up and then back across ...

'There!' she says aloud to herself as she spots Max in the eighth row, fourth one over.

'Alex!'

She looks up as she hears a familiar voice call her from across the platform.

Nat waving on the other side of the circular steel ring. He has made it to the roof too, another door to another stairwell behind him. She looks around but can't see Thackeray.

Alex circles the platform, circling above the tournament floor and below the top of the cone-shaped Citadel. And it is as if she is standing still, and the strength in her step and heart are turning the world beneath. Their world is turning, and it is not going back.

She looks up at the inverted cone hanging over the centre of the tournament floor and the siren and scoreboard dangling from it. Her eyes travel further up into the narrowing space where the cone's cable is bolted to the roof.

'Alex!'

Nat calls again from the stairwell to the tenth floor above.

'Go!' she shouts. 'Go, I'll be right there. Get ready ... we'll be right there. Behind you.'

Thackeray is up further on the roof, crouched, tying the cords.

'Where are they?' he cries.

Nat doesn't answer him. He looks back at Alex and tosses her the firing half of the rifle. He goes to help Thackeray prepare.

The rifle hits the platform near her feet with a clatter, but instead of picking it up, she starts climbing. Standing on the hand railing surrounding the platform, she reaches above her head to a structural beam. Her stomach tightens. The steel beam runs straight to the tip of the building, and she knows she can shimmy along it, straight to the siren's bolted-mounting. She pulls her legs up and holds her weight with hands and feet wrapping the beam. The steel feels warm to the touch from the sun.

One hand over the other, she pulls herself out over the Arena floor. Not looking down, she moves far enough to reach the cable. She takes a breath and lets her head hang back. The floor below looms into her eyesight, far further down than she would like.

'Never look down,' she reminds herself.

Her hands weaken. She thinks of the rifle back on the platform. And she thinks ... she needs leverage. She looks up at the loop screwed into the roof which holds the cable and cone below it. She needs to go back. Using the rifle, she might be able to loosen the loop and drop everything, the cone, the siren, the scoreboard onto the Arena and the glass floor below.

Chapter 11

Shattered Glass

The guard strides between their table and the next, staring at them as he does. In his eyes, Max sees disgust. Max feels as if his world has turned upside-down. He thinks of chess, the tournament and life in a way he has never before. He lifts his eyes from the board, and meets his opponent's eyes. The board is not worthy of their attention. They each value the person across the table far more.

There is no more tapping. The tapping has passed. The boy has warned Max not to win the game. In doing so, he has warned him about the incineration room.

It is Max's move.

He raises his arm, passes it over the board, his fingers hovering over the pieces. Then Max knows what to do. He extends his hand further, gripping Conor's shoulder.

'Let's get these people out of here,' Max says.

The baton-wielding guard strides back up between the tables behind Max. Max only knows something coming for him by the fear in the boy's eyes.

—

On her second go, Alex slides the rifle from the back of her waistband. She begins threading it, slim end first, through the loop of the cable mount with while sitting on the structural beam, gripping it with her thighs. Pulling with one hand and pushing with the other, she tries to fracture the loop bearing everything below it. Her trunk twists and tightens; she might just break before it does.

Her face reddens, her arms weaken, and sweat builds. The bracket into the roof holding the loop twists. At the moment it does, Alex feels a tooth crack under the force of her clenching. The pain distracts her. She twists again and the bracket spins free and swings precariously.

But the sudden jerk unbalances her, and she topples, but manages to grab the rifle strap above her, but the gun is already sliding from the dangling loop. The yellow petals she concealed at Sarah's grave rain from her pocket and float to the Arena floor below.

—

It all happens too fast. Max sees the guard extend his baton and place it to Conor's head. In front of Max, the boy's eyes roll upward in their sockets and vibrate in a side-to-side before he falls to the ground.

Max jumps up, staring in disbelief as a stream of blood trickles from the boy's eyes. The players at the tables nearby rise from their seats. Screams and chaos fill the room, and the people run panicked, looking for escape.

As Max turns, the guard grips him by the neck with one hand and brings the baton towards him. As the current lights up blue in Max's face, he sees yellow petals floating down from above.

—

Winston looks down at the shreds of paper littered over him and picks the pieces off himself. Skinner slides the letter opener from his waistband, and Winston sees the flash before he feels it. Skinner is light and fast as he rams it into the old man's stomach.

Winston looks down at the hand still against his stomach, and feels the warmth of his own blood overflowing from his bottom lip. He looks at his own hand and the shred of paper in it containing the words.

Thou shalt not kill.

He holds Skinner's hand at his gut with one hand. With the other, he holds the piece of the journal to Skinner's face with a bloodied smile.

'I've been really thinking about this one,' he says.

Skinner tries to pull his hand back, but Winston fights to hold it. He pinches another piece of torn paper from his chest,

'As for this one,' Winston begins, 'Matthew 7:26. You're gonna know all about this one. Quite soon, I think.'

Winston's eyes feel heavy. He fights the weight that seems to be pulling his eyelids closed. The elevator door slides open and behind Skinner, he sees a crowded floor. But when his eyes close, Winston sees a tunnel. He squints down this narrow tunnel. At the open end, far ahead, he sees a warm light. A figure steps into the light with a humped four-legged shape. He can discern the silhouette of a woman holding the reins of a camel-shape. They stand there, waiting patiently as statues.

—

Alex dangles from rifle's strap, watching the rifle barrel slip back out of the loop. She tries to reach the roof beam with her other arm but the movement causes the rifle to free itself quicker. Only her fingertips touch the beam, and they're not enough to hold her weight.

The loosened bracket begins to creak and unscrew and Alex is swung by the momentum of the bracket, the loop and the cable dropping. Everything above her is unthreading and she sinks lower, further from the beam. Alex makes one desperate effort to climb the rifle's strap and raise herself to the beam. Alex pulls herself up as hard as she can and as one hand clasps around the beam, the rifle strap falls freely from her other hand and the cable and bracket are whipped down past her eyes, and everything, the cone, the siren and the giant scoreboard are falling for the Arena floor.

—

Max sees the glowing circles of guard's baton twist and turn, and beyond them he sees flower petals. He recognises the petals as ones from yellow daffodil flowers, the ones Grandad gifted to him in his mother's name every birthday.

A memory whispers into Max's ear. The clock ticks, and the boy taps. Black and white. Tick, tap, black, white, tick, tap, black, white, tick, tap, black, white ...

Grandad? Mam? Alex? Anyone? Please, I don't know what to do.

He hears his grandad's voice. *Your loved ones, Max, dead or alive, have a habit of showing up when you need them. Showing you the way. You just have to be willing to hear them.*

The world turns slowly and the guard grips Max's head, wrenching his neck back, so he sees petals floating down from above. Amid the circling glow from the baton and the petals, Max sees the scoreboard break free from the roof above. Max pulls himself to the present and pushes the guard back, back, back. The guard stumbles onto the Arena floor, releasing his hold of Max who snatches the limp arms of his friend and moves faster and stronger than he ever thought possible, dragging Conor along with him. The loud explosion of crashing glass and metal pursues him even as he powers through a straight row between the tables – ripples of destruction following both boys.

Max feels the power of the crash beneath his fleeing feet. The Arena floor splinters underneath as the weight of the cone and everything in the roof of the Citadel tears a gaping hole in the glass floor. Max drags the boy onto his shoulder as the hole grows wider and wider, an invisible power eating away more and more of the floor. The growing hole chases Max's heels as he runs, as tables, chairs, boards, pieces and the floor itself tumble and crash through levels below the Arena.

Max runs for the stability of the outer wall, hoping that some floor will remain. He takes his eyes off his footing to look behind, and instantly he regrets it. The glass underneath his shoe sole slides back from underneath him. He throws himself forward sliding on the flat of his chest, with an inert Conor on his back.

The cone is still eating its way down through the glass floors below but the hole it has left in the Arena floor is wide and still growing. A large crack runs across the floor, heading straight for Max. And then his entire body's weight drops leaving his breath and his heartbeat somewhere above him. As he falls, he reaches up, desperate to catch hold of someone or anything before it's too late.

—

Skinner exits the elevator, leaving Winston's lifeless body occupying it. Nothing moves but the old man's whispering lips.

'Matthew 7:24 Everyone then who hears these words of mine and does them will be like a wise man who built his house on the rock.

'Matthew 7:26 And everyone who hears these words of mine and does not do them will be like a foolish man who built his house on the sand.'

—

Three-quarters of the Arena floor is gone, shattered. Below it, the roof cone is now wedged in the fifth floor. On the shattered levels below, laboratories, offices and canteens are smashed, filled with remnants of glass and steel and torn cabling. APZON staff call for help. A sparking cable has started a fire on the floor two levels below where Max dangles from the eighth floor over the burning pit. Conor's grip of his hand is all that saves him from oblivion. Conor is blinded but lies on the shattered glass, holding on to the friend he fell with.

'Max!'

As Max hears a voice calling his name, he feels himself pulled dragged back onto the Arena floor by the boy. The pair scramble to safety nearer the outer wall on their bellies.

—

Alex hangs from the roof by one hand and then two. She swings her legs up, grateful to rest her arms and peers down into the cone of destruction below her.

—

'Max!'

He hears the voice again as he gasps for breath, his and Conor's backs against the wall.

'Max!'

Max looks up to see Alex high above him. He glances at Conor, but realises he cannot see her. He can see nothing, so he will have to be the eyes for the boy who has saved his life. Looking up, he can see Alex is pointing at something opposite her but at what, Max doesn't know.

Alex makes her way from the beam back to the platform. She smashes her elbow against the emergency glass of a fire-hose reel and nurses her arm from the botched effort. Irritated, she picks up a shattered piece of metal debris from the floor and flings it at the glass. This time it shatters, and she reaches in to pull the fire hose free.

The nozzle of the fire hose swings down and crashes against the wall above Max and Conor. Max cranes his neck out and can see the other end is wound around the railing above and joined to the reel mounted beside Alex on the floor above. The nozzle swings just out of Max and Conor's reach.

'Listen, Conor, I'm gonna lift you up to reach a rope, a hose. Grab it when you feel it.'

Max helps Conor up to reach it. Conor grips it with one hand and both legs and reaches back for Max's hand. But Max is torn from the hand of the boy above him by a strong grip on his legs.

Conor swings out wider, out over the gaping hole, reaching out into fresh air for Max's hand.

'Go! Keep climbing!' Max yells while on the flat of his back. 'Get outta here while you can. Climb, Conor. Go!'

Max has no idea who this man is. A man who tore him from his escape, flung him to the ground and now has a foot upon his chest. But he sees disgust in his eyes.

'Self-sacrifice. Emotion. You see that's why we could never go in mass production with your type,' the man says. 'Emotions are too erratic.'

Max crawls backwards, away from the man, before getting back to his feet. A shorn cable showers sparks of hot light. Shards of glass fall from the ceiling above and land shattering in the space between Max and Skinner.

'Your grandad really left you in the dark, didn't he?'

'My grandad taught me everything I know.'

'But he didn't tell you he killed your mother, did he?'

—

Conor reaches the railings above, following Alex's encouraging voice. Then the building itself drops with a shudder under its own weight, its frame failing. With the jerk, Alex is thrown and the boy who saved the life of her friend is flung from the railing. Alex hand reaches out and feels the breath pulled from her body as the boy falls backwards. Soundless, touching nothing, Conor falls – down into the ever-growing tornado of flames below. Alex reels. This boy who Max tried to save, is gone. She feels the loss and guilt. She never wants to lose like this again.

A spiderweb of glass surrounds the vast cone and siren on the fifth floor until with one more shattering crack, the entire level disintegrates, and everything falls through to the next floor and the flames reach higher.

She throws her leg over the railing, and grabs the fire hose to lower herself, one exhausted arm's length at a time towards Max.

Skinner leans his weight into the baton and pushes it towards Max's face. Max tries to wrench it away. The baton sparks, a bolt of blue crackles of death between its two poles. And behind the blue, Skinner smiles in anticipation. Max pushes back but Skinner's weight is too much, and Max closes his eyes as the blue light closes in on him. The weight lifts from him with the sound of a thud and a crack. He opens his eyes again.

'You OK, kiddo?' says Grandad.

The old man stands with his back to him, brandishing the empty half rifle like a bat. He glances over his shoulder at Max, keeping an eye on Skinner.

Skinner is on the ground, nursing his shoulder, and Grandad remains in batting stance, ready to strike again. The building cracks, releasing a side of the glass walling opposite them. It falls to the ground surrounding the Citadel. Max gets to his feet and wraps his arms around the old man and inhales that familiar scent.

Winston points upwards as Alex swings from the fire hose over their heads.

'Get up there. Go with Alex,' he instructs Max, stepping towards Skinner, ready to swing again. The wind blowing through the building's exposed side, picks up.

'What about you?' Max says. 'I'm staying with you. How are you getting out of here?'

Grandad's eyes are firmly on Skinner.

'Max, you are going to take Alex's hand, climb up and get out of here. You remember what I told you if anything ever happens to me?'

Grandad reaches back for Max and pulls him closer.

'Chess is supposed to emulate war,' the old man whispers. 'You can fight a war with your head or your heart. Rarely both. The hard part is choosing.'

Winston smiles encouragingly and taps his finger against his own temple.

'Those who fight with their head often win by refusing to let emotions influence decisions.'

He touches his chest where his old heart beats and leans in, speaking with urgency now.

'You're a very unique boy, Max, capable of greatness. An unprecedented mind, capable of things never seen before. But there is also a part of you that is heart. Real heart and human emotion. At some point, you will have to choose. Follow your head. Or listen to your heart.

'Choose the real in you or the artificial. That choice will be hard. And you will be the first to make it. You will decide what the future will be.'

His old hand touches Max's soft young one.

'You're always gonna face choices, but please listen to your heart too.'

Max grasps his Grandad's hand, tight in his own.

'I am, and you're coming with us.'

Grandad shakes his hand free from Max's hold and wraps the boy under his arm.

'We have to sacrifice some pieces in order to save others,' he says. 'No one piece is more important than another, Max. Only time is important. Time can defeat a full board. Time is the only truly valuable resource. You'll understand in time.'

Winston slides the pen from his sleeve and presses it in Max's hand.

'You write your own ending.'

Grandad lifts Max up high enough for Alex to reach him from where she hangs. She holds on to Max as Grandad lets him go. The old man vanishes as soon as Alex's gaze meets Max's eyes. Max grabs hold of the fire hose himself, and they climb. Swaying gently as the destruction continues on all their sides.

Skinner is back on his feet as soon as Grandad lifts Max to safety with Alex. Max looks down to see his Grandad wrestle Skinner again while his tears rain down on them. But Max climbs onwards.

—

Skinner presses the baton close to Winston's cheek, but the old man rolls to one side, and both men tumble. Winston manages to elbow Skinner's face, and gets to his feet. But as soon as he turns he gets a fist in his injured stomach. Grandad bends double, and Skinner sparks the baton in his hand and hits him.

Winston vibrates for moments as the electricity fills him. He falls to his knees before the tyrant and the bolts running through him finally end. Skinner brings the baton to Winston's head, to the father of the woman he has loved and the woman who this old man dared take back from him.

With one finger, Skinner sends the blue bolt through whatever Winston thinks, burning the thoughts, the memories and the past continuously until little is left. When Skinner releases the baton, the old man slides lifeless to the floor, blood seeping from his nose.

Skinner drags a table, screeching across the floor. Swiping the board and its pieces aside, he clambers onto it. Reaching for the hose end swinging above his head, he begins to climb after Max.

—

Alex crawls over the top of railing first, followed by Alex. Falling onto the platform floor, they hear Nat calling out. They see him shout from the steps leading to the roof. Nat vanishes from Alex and Max's sight. He doesn't wait for an answer. He has to prepare.

Alex gets up to follow but hears Max's breathless gasp. She watches him being pulled back over the top of the railing by Skinner's blood-covered arm.

Alex watches Max's feet lift off the ground, raising slowly off the platform as if in another time and reality. She reaches out, feeling her arms heavier than they ever have been. She feels weighted. She does not want to lose another from her hand's reach. And certainly not Max. Yet, Skinner drags Max backwards over the railing.

Chapter 12

The Story Passes On

In mid-air, Max stops falling. And then, back, back, he moves until his feet are back on the platform. He is out of Skinner's arms. Then Alex and he go backwards over the railing and down the fire hose, they lower themselves as the sun spins back on its axis and sound whirrs.

Max is back below, embracing his grandad. Conor flies closer to Alex's hands; maybe close enough for her to reach him this time. The siren reverses out of the hole, and the damage becomes undone. Max retakes his seat in the eighth row, and the tournament rewinds – faster, much faster – than it played out. And faster still, the sun shoots back across the sky, and shadows spin around their fulcrums.

Then the guard, cabin, home, blood and the camel. Winston pulls Max off Lumpy after the boy shoots him. Then blood, the blood, blood and more blood. And now he watches himself stay as Max runs away. Just as he did then.

As a spectator, our mistakes are easier to admit. Winston screams at his past self – to turn back and spend every moment with the boy. Winston vowed to be by this child's side until his own dying day. It would take 13 years. Winston sees Max's scream in eerie silence now. Something is broken.

Winston will not see the end of the tunnel. In death, our memories disperse and are free. And the images and memories like photographs continue to flick by. Digging the ground for his daughter's grave, pages from her blank journals. Raise the boy right, morals, choose heart over head, human over machine, logic, technology, art, literature, give the boy stories, literature, parables. He will choose humanity.

Try to recall and rewrite Mockingbirds, Tales of Two Cities, Wizards in Oz, Thou shalt not ... Frankenstein's monster; The Mustang hidden in the forest floor bunker, the air ducts, help on the way, the mornings, the evenings, the nights and the years.

The pages of his daughter's journals flick and flitter past his eyes. The words he has written in them flash back and then faster, and Winston can hear the flicking and feel the air they fan back onto his face. Then he is submerged in the cold lake, and his skin grips tighter onto every part of him. He can see it all in parts. He is seeing it all back; seeing what he has seen then but now from different eyes.

He hears Max's voice, his own too, the flicking of pages, splash, the rifle click. He sees the 'camel protein' escape, realises the boy knows how to play chess from birth.

And now the trees fill his eyes. He watches the brown leaves turn green and grow back as the years flick back with the pages. Queens and pawns. Soup steaming and a pot in the corner of the cabin billowing a smelly vegetable cloud; the warm aroma between Max's nose and the book on the floor.

Winston stands outside; his home not yet built. The darkness of the night has surrounded the moon in the sky. Nightmarish, picturesque.

A bolt of lightning cracks, ripping a line through the picture. The bolt vanishes before eyes have seen it, and then just as quick, the picture is undamaged but impermanently so. Always impermanently. Lightning will always strike again.

Memories come that are unfamiliar. Unwatched, unfelt and for a long time hidden, he will see them now. Maybe forever. Winston has never forgotten. He misses her constantly. They were so close, father and daughter, as she grew before his eyes.

His Arizona princess girl forever.

But little girls grow up. They become women. And they meet men.

Winston dying eyes open.

—

Max opens his eyes and meets Alex's terrified ones. Something is being taken away from her. Something important; something she loves. Her arm is outstretched, and her hand is closing in a grasp; she is reaching for his.

He feels the weight of Skinner on his back. Clawing at him, pulling him over the railing. But it happens slowly. And Max now feels time's weight coming back.

Click.

Alex clenches her teeth. She will not allow this breath be taken from her. Not this one, not this time. Not again. She reaches out for Max's leg. And she catches it. Upside down, disoriented, Max feels himself slam against the outer side of the railing.

She holds him, struggling because Skinner's vice grip on Max is adding to the weight. As Max's t-shirt shreds in Skinner's hold, the tyrant scrambles up his body like a centipede. Skinner gets his hands onto the railing.

Max feels his hair hang below his head and blood fill up behind his face. His cheeks droop towards his eyes. He imagines seeing his grandad.

The building shunts again, and the fire hose reel comes free from the wall. The hose falls, a sudden weightlessness, and then a jerk. The stop has a sharp snap as the reel catches on the railings, smashing into the railing beside Skinner.

Winston's eyes open amid the destruction around him. He manages to escape the chaotic stream of memory. Beside him, he sees the broken rifle, and he reaches for it.

Alex summons her strength and begins to pull Max to safety over the railings. Skinner snatches at him with one free hand again. He is determined to pull the boy from Alex's clutches and fling him into the fires below.

Winston rummages in his left pants pocket, then his right. Empty. But it's there inside his breast pocket. The brass is warm. The third bullet. The bullet he took from the boy's pocket the night of his thirteenth birthday. This number thirteen might just be lucky.

He touches it as the hose reel comes free over the railing. Plummeting for the brittle last of Arena floor, it falls like a deadweight, set to smash the last of the floor that Winston lies upon.

The alloy reel's descent races against the loading of the brass bullet in the barrel. Click. The reel's impact shatters the entirety of the remaining floor. The rifle's stump flips up behind the barrel as Winston descends, and bang!

One remaining bullet. One shot. One chance.

The bullet reaches its target and Skinner falls but snatches a handful of Max's hair. For a millisecond, he rejoices in saving himself. Then the hair rips from Max's head and Skinner tumbles loose. Fire fills the hole that has eaten through the centre of the building, eating the building from the inside out, and Skinner tumbles into the burning heart of his creation.

But Max only sees Grandad in the flames. He feels the sudden heat on his face as the old man's body adds to the fire and the flames soar upwards below him.

—

Winston sees Max's scream in eerie silence. Something is broken. Winston will not see the end of the tunnel. In death, our memories disperse and are free. And the images and memories like photographs continue to flick by. Digging the ground for his daughter's grave, pages from her blank journals. Raise the boy right, morals, choose heart over head, human over machine, logic, technology, art, literature, give the boy stories, literature, parables. He will choose humanity.

Try to recall and rewrite Mockingbirds, Tales of Two Cities, Wizards in Oz, Thou shalt not ... Frankenstein's monster; The Mustang hidden in the forest floor bunker, the air ducts, help on the way, the mornings, the evenings, the nights and the years.

The pages of his daughter's journals flick and flitter past his eyes. The words he has written in them flash back and then faster, and Winston can hear the flicking and feel the air they fan back onto his face. Then he is submerged in the cold lake, and his skin grips tighter onto every part of him. He can see it all in parts. He is seeing it all back; seeing what he has seen then but now from different eyes.

He hears Max's voice, his own too, the flicking of pages, splash, the rifle click. He sees the protein camel escape, realises the boy knows how to play chess from birth.

And now the trees fill his eyes. He watches the brown leaves turn green and grow back as the years flick back with the pages. Soup steaming. Queens and pawns, a pot in the corner of the cabin billowing a smelly vegetable cloud; the warm aroma between Max's nose and the book on the floor in front of his younger self.

Winston stands outside; his home not yet built. The darkness of the night has surrounded the moon in the sky. Nightmarish, picturesque.

A bolt of lightning cracks, ripping a line through the picture. The bolt vanishes before eyes have seen it, and then just as quick, the picture is undamaged but impermanently so. Always impermanently. Lightning will always strike again.

Memories come that are unfamiliar. Unwatched, unfelt and for a long time hidden, he will see them now. Maybe forever. Winston has never forgotten. He misses her constantly. They were so close, father and daughter, as she grew before his eyes.

His Arizona princess girl forever.

But little girls grow up. They become women. And they meet men.

He begins to realise he lives only in these memories now.

—

Max gets a grip of the railing and climbs back over, leaving Alex slump to the floor completely drained. He wraps his arms around her and pulls her to her feet, and they hold each other for a moment. The moment must be brief. The building drops again, and tilts to one side. Hurriedly, they run up the stairs to the roof as the building crumbles under their feet.

The cool open air touches their warm faces, and they focus on the sight of Nat and Thackeray across the rooftop. Thackeray uses the three-digit code Winston gave him, and that extends a helipad from the side of the building. It will be their runway for take-off.

The building's slant increases as Max and Alex approach, but they run harder, chasing behind Thackeray and Nat with the wind-sails. The four head for the roof's edge.

Thackeray struggles to hold his glider at the right angle. Alex and Max catch up to him. He has to move quicker if he is to make it off this roof. Alex grabs Thackeray's hand and his glider as she passes. She runs for the edge of the sloping roof, and Thackeray races with her. They leap onto the ledge and off the building's side, madly throwing themselves with a fool's trust in the wind.

Max chases after Nat, metres behind and catches up with him as Nat's feet lift off the roof. Max springs forward with him, entering into the nothingness beyond the building's roof, but he misses the glider and clutches fresh air. Closing his eyes, he finds the safety of familiar blackness there.

He hears the sound of the structure finally falling below him, crashing back down into its own foundations, burning in sand-fanned flames. The darkness remains behind Max's eyes as he falls.

In the laboratory of a satellite APZON building, new AI-bio hybrid clones lie immersed in clear fluid. One new Skinner and multiple Hitchcocks float among other almost fully completed adult bodies.

Chapter 13

The End of the Board

Winston drove the Mustang through the wall six days ago. The wall is smaller back then. Everything inside Skinner's Utopian dream is in its early stages. Winston has military training and has lived nomadically before. Survival is never going to be a great stretch of his resolve. Worry is his only difficulty. It has been six days, and he has not seen or heard any sign of her.

'She says she's coming here. She'll come.'

The words have become a mantra and a comfort of sorts while he waits day after day at the rendezvous. Winston hates his instinctual distrust.

What if she changes her mind again and stays, goes back to be with Adam? What if she can't get away from him? What if something has happened to her? What if he isn't at the right spot in this 'forest'?

He tries but cannot control his thoughts, his mind, his questioning. His knowledge of the compound has proved undeniably useful. He has made use of one of the bunkers along the oxygen line for his shelter. It is the smallest of them and is buried under the foot of the mountain rock.

It has never been used. He knows nobody but the architect will know its location. Maybe the builders will remember it too. But he hopes to be gone soon, accompanied by his daughter. He will not be staying long in this horrible place, so there is no need to make it a home.

In another world, another life, it might make a nice place there by the lake. Standing by the water, sometimes he believes it is real. He knows better. But what is real? It is water. Water anywhere is still water. Yes, the lake has not naturally formed there, but does that make it fake?

On the sixth day, Winston sees the first sign of life. A small electric vehicle hums out from the trees. Skinner showed him the early designs. Maybe the 'eccentric billionaire' isn't so crazy after all. Crouched and hidden, Winston watches the E.V. until it stops. Awkwardly braking and stopping, the driver pushes the door open.

Uuuhhhh!

He hears a loud moaning from inside. Winston slips closer, staying low and keeping out of sight, he moves through the trees. What is it? A pain-filled creature is calling out.

Uuuhhhh! Aaahhhhh!

Now Winston knows what…who it is. He moves fast, jumping branches, handspringing over a rock to reach the E.V. Getting to his daughter is all that matters; the only reason he has come here. Her leg is the first he sees of her, dangling out the door. She wails, and the only person she really wants is there. Her father appears by the vehicle's open door. She feels like a little girl again, calling for his help. This is not how she wants him to see her. No little girl wants their father in their birthing room, yet she feels safe for the first time in a long time.

Winston instinctively starts to help, but his hands are quickly bloodied by her waters.

'Sarah!'

'Dad, I'm sorry, I'm sorry…I should have told you but….'

Winston takes a steely breath and talks confidently.

'No, my girl, don't worry about anything else now. I'm here, and I'm gonna make sure you're OK, and this baby will be OK, and we're getting three of us out of here. You'll never have to see him ever again or this place. You're safe now with me. I'll never let him near …'

'I'm sorry, Dad, I should have listened to you.'

Winston is busy.

'Dad, I don't know what it is. What this is…what Adam has put inside of me.'

Winston wonders if her temperature is too high, but he has not enough hands for the multitude of tasks requested of them.

'Dad, I don't want this thing. This isn't my… '

Sarah cries red-faced and sweating.

'This is his, Dad. He put something inside me. Dad, I don't want this thing. This thing isn't human. Get it out of me. Stop it!'

But her head bobs back lifeless as the pain overcomes her. His mind hears her words over and over as he works, but there is a lot to do if he is to save both of them.

—

The blackness behind Max's eyes remains until he feels the sudden jerk of his arm being caught. Gravity and momentum shunts his shoulder as it whips in pain. His eyes open to see Nat above him in the glider. He lifts his legs just in time to avoid the treetops below him, and pulls himself to the underside of the glider. His sudden weight has jerked the glider down on one side and they cross the trees fast, heading toward the hard foot of the mountain, losing altitude fast.

Another glider, with Alex and Thackeray dangling beneath, cuts through the sky, watching above.

Behind them, the APZON building continues to crumble and smoke, caving in on itself. The Citadel had consumed itself already when Grandad's homemade fuel explodes in the boot of the Mustang. Grandad needed to be certain.

Suddenly, Nat and Max are out of the trees. The glider streams into a clearing out the back of the forest, and the light and sudden brightness below their feet is instinctively reassuring. Alex and Thackeray are close behind them.

The setting sun looks across the lake top as they fly over it. The water shimmers, and a cold freshness comes from its surface. Alex looks ahead. They are over water for now but not for long. The lake comes up to meet them fast.

Thackeray lets go, drops into the water and hits it at a sprawling angle. Alex abandons the glider too and hits the water further up from her co-pilot. The wind whips the remaining glider into a corkscrew descent flinging Max towards the water and Nat and the glider towards the land.

—

At the narrowest point of Winston's tunnel, a memory reel flickers. Some remnants from a life. It isn't until the baby drops into Winston's hands, then cries, that he realises it has been silent in the car for some time. Sarah is not awake.

Initially, he thinks she must be unconscious. It is a boy as we already know well, and Winston struggles to wrap this fragile, slippery bundle and keep him warm. The baby is screaming at him. Baby. He has not got a name yet. His mother will give him one when she comes to.

Now, her dad and her son just lie together in the back of the Pawn, waiting for her to wake. Then they can get out of this place. The Pawn is spacious enough for Winston to lie near her and the baby. But he will not lie for long. He cannot. They will come looking for the Pawn and Sarah.

Winston looks between the seats at the ornament, a pawn, made of wood and encircled in a silver ring. It swings on the rear-view mirror. And Winston holds the baby and knows he will be by this child's side forever. And never leave him to be alone.

—

Small circles chase out larger ones, spreading wider and wider towards the edges until the ripples are spent and the lake is glasslike again after their plunging impacts. Max and Thackeray wade heavily to the lakeside, dragging heavy clothes with them. They can see Alex wring water from her hair ahead of them.

On the bank, they remove waterlogged layers in the red glow of the evening.

Alex notes Max has emerged from the water with a large white patch of skin surrounding his left eye and cheek. Thackeray sees it too. But Max only feels what may be adrenaline coming to rest in his stomach. He is shaken inside. But he and his friends are by the lake and the back of Alex's hand touches the back of his.

A cloud of black and red smoke billows somewhere beyond the trees. The burning glow from the Citadel flickers large in a silence beyond the treeline. Max looks in disbelief at the altered skyline. The towering Citadel is already only a memory. The sunset lines the cloud in a red glow, and the three watch.

'Home by sundown,' says Alex, nudging Max's elbow with hers.

They smile in relieved silence until all three look around them.

'Where's Nat?'

—

When they find it, the three have little time to comprehend their friend's lifeless figure at the bottom of the tree. They see two Patrol trucks approach in the distance, and the lights of another comes between the trees.

'We have to get out of here,' says Alex.

'But Nat. He can't be gone, can he?'

Thackeray is the last to relinquish hope as Max tries to steer him towards the bunker.

But Alex is defiant.

'No, Max. This way,' she says, pointing in the opposite direction. 'I'm not hiding. I'm not going home to close the door. I'm getting out of here, out of this place. I'll never know the whole truth ... unless I can see outside.'

Alex speaks with a certainty that Max feels no need to question.

'I feel the woman knew more, had so much more to tell me ... but I had to leave,' said Alex already driving her way up the hill.

'The woman?' Max queries as he follows, dragging Thackeray. 'Who are you talking about?'

'A woman. A scientist,' says Alex, trying to remember if the woman in the white coat had a name. 'A woman who worked in the APZON building.'

Alex points back to where the Citadel stood before realising.

'I met her on one of the levels as I climbed up through the building.'

'Why are we listening to APZON employees?' demands Thackeray.

They stop to hide in a copse of trees as the patrol cars pass.

'It wasn't like that. I don't think she was an employee. She showed me things. She told me things.'

Alex feels the vial she was given inside her pocket.

'She knew your Mam.'

Max doesn't respond.

'She wasn't lying ... I think ... she's worth trusting. Besides, none of us have ever been outside this town, and she told me we need to, to know ... I don't know what, but something. Don't you guys at least wanna see?'

The three dart across the road after the patrol cars disappear, dropping, one after the other, into the ditch on the other side.

'What about everyone in the village… and what about your dad?' Thackeray says.

Alex looks at both Alex and Thackeray and feels fondness and fear.

'They will never leave. They haven't yet. No one has, and they're never going to.'

Again, Alex mistakenly looks for the Citadel.

'After APZON and Skinner took everything from them – their jobs, their homes, their ability to buy food or clothing. They never left. They just stay here and take it.'

Alex lets a moment pass before finishing.

'They haven't left yet. And I think it's because they have left something – somewhere – to come here. That's where we should be. That's where we need to go. Or at least see.

'Our true home might be outside of here. And we have the right to choose as they did. Either way, I'm sure this place is bad, and we need to get out of here.'

The eye within Alex's mind replays the images and the words of the woman in the science lab.

'Do you know what an electrolyte is? The human body contains many. After death, the solidification of the body produces a residue that has a unique blend of our electrolytes. This electrolyte blend is useful in battery manufacturing.'

The white-coated woman had stumbled over her words then.

'But people take too long to die, let alone solidify. And Skinner wants to keep his society ignorant; he needs to eliminate the intelligent.'

Alex remembers how the woman's eyes remained closed.

'Two birds, one stone ... three, actually. Human electrolytes have been found to speed up the growth of plant life too.'

Alex cannot even bear to repeat her words to anyone. The woman who shares the horrible secrets of their world does so without realising Alex will never speak of them again.

'Alex is right,' Max says. 'They'll never leave.'

'Is that a yes?' Alex asks, surprised. 'Are we getting out of here?'

The door to the place which Max and his grandfather called home is still visible from where they are.

'I don't have anything to stay for,' Max says.

'That's two of us,' adds Thackeray. 'I've never had a mam or a dad.'

Thackeray's eyes appear fixed on the mud at his feet, but his voice does not sound as sad as one might expect to hear a person saying these words.

'But the people in the village are the closest I've ever had to a family.'

'We won't ask you to leave,' says Max, 'if you don't think it's the right thing to do.'

'Aborigines,' says Thackeray, confusing his two friends. 'Do you guys know the Aborigines? I don't know if they are real stories or not. Bennie in the village tells me about them. I like them anyway.

'They were a group of people kinda like us. They lived without technology on this massive ... Anyway, the Aborigines, when they got to a certain a age they would just walk. They'd go out into the wilderness alone ... these kids ... would just go and test the skills they had learned and learn new ones to survive. I bet they learned really quick that way.

'They'd just stay out there until they were done. It might take months, it might take years, but they'd just stay until they knew they were done. Until they had found what they were looking for.'

Alex and Max watch and listen with admiration.

'I wish I had that kind of courage,' Thackeray says. 'But I don't think I do.'

A guard shouts at them from through the trees and yells to alert his colleagues.

Alex goes to move, but Max stops her.

'We could drive. My grandad showed me a place where he has hidden a car. He has told me to go there if anything ever happens to him.'

'The Mustang?'

Alex's reply surprises him.

'How do you know about that?'

'That's how ... your grandad got us into the APZON building. He crashed the Mustang into the lobby of the Citadel with explosives liquid stuff he mixed in its trunk.'

Max tries to centre his thoughts.

'Why would he show me that place? Tell me to go there if anything goes wrong, and then take the only thing worth anything and burn it to a crisp? Why show it to me at all?'

—

A breeze whips through the Mustang's old housing space.

—

'I don't know, Max,' says Alex, taking his hand.

'When we realised you'd been taken to APZON, your grandad was stressed. We didn't really have a lot of options. I guess his priority then was to get you back and worry about a new getaway car later.'

'So we walk?' Thackeray asks. 'That's crazy. It's dangerous and destined to fail. We should go back to the village.'

'We walk,' said Max. 'Just like the Arabrigbys.'

'That's Aborigines,' laughs Thackeray.

'We mightn't have to walk,' said Alex and she nods to something half-concealed by trees in the distance. 'Anybody know how to drive one of those?'

Max recognises it instantly

'It's the Pawn 1!'

'The what?'

Alex and Thackeray chase after him.

—

'SEARCH THE WHOLE PERIMETER!' a voice bellows through the trees as all three slip into the car and Max pulls the doors closed. Even though Max knows the battery on the Pawn must be old, he has confidence in it.

More voices of APZON guards all over the forest echo through the place all carrying silver moulded rifles rather than the taser-batons carried by guards in the Citadel.

'We have to get out of here now,' Alex whispers as Max turns the key.

The Pawn 1 starts and Max is grateful EVs run silently.

One guard, who has strayed from the group, stands watching the trees in the distance. Max's home burns over the guard's shoulder. He notices the tyre tracks in the mud.

—

Driving through the city draws many eyes as the car is old. Max drives while the others rest, but they pass through U City without incident.

Alex lies in the car holding the vial. She only sleeps intermittently, and each time she opens her eyes, she gazes upon Max's profile. She thinks about the other Max – the empty-eyed one in the Citadel – and closes her own eyes again.

Beyond the city is vast stretches of desert. The road ahead is straight, freshly painted and smells of warms tarmac. It is empty and unused. They travel alone with only tumbleweed moving with them towards the ever-vanishing horizon. Until they cannot go any further. The engine cuts out, and the Pawn rolls to an eventual stop. Max is the first to get out.

It has been hours since the Citadel fell, and far back on the horizon, spires of smoke still rise into the sky. They have seen no sign of patrols on this road. It's as if the guards have no concern for this area outside the U City.

Thackeray wakes on the back seat and spots Max outside.

'Will you get back in here before a patroller sees ...?'

'They won't see,' says Max. 'I don't think they patrol out here. There's no point in patrolling it.'

Blocking the sun with his hand, he looks as far into the distance as his eyes will allow.

'Nobody in their right mind would walk…' he says, almost to himself.

'So why aren't we driving?' says Alex, stretching as she gets out.

'Because it stops here. The cars must take their charge from under the road, and it stops here.'

Max smiles.

'That's why Grandad wanted to find a fuel that would power the petrol engine. There is no vehicle inside that city that can go any further than here.'

The city lights begin to wake as evening falls.

'They don't want anyone inside to go any further.'

'Yes, your grandad wasn't drinking the alcohol,' says Alex. 'He was searching for a fuel to replace the petrol.'

—

After spending a night in the car, the morning walk through the desert is almost welcome. Two hours pass, but they see nothing but dry, dusty soil as far as the eye can see. Max realises they might tire long before this road does. For now the road continues, and so do they.

'How far are we planning to walk, Alex?' says Thackeray, exasperated.

'Until we reach something.'

'Guys…' says Max.

'What if we never reach something?' says Thackeray.

'We have to meet something.'

'Guys…'

'That woman only said there was something out here we have to see. What if she was lying?'

'Guys ...'

Max is louder each time he interrupts.

'She wasn't lying, but I didn't have time to find out more ...'

'GUYS!' Max shouts.

'Jeez! What?' says Alex.

'What's that?' says Max, looking into the distant horizon between Alex and Thackeray.

Alex uses her hand to shade her eyes from the sun.

'What's what?' she asks.

'That!'

He points again.

'That's the horizon.'

'No. I think it's ...'

Every direction they look, it's out there. They walk for another hour before it becomes clear what it is. They need to touch it before they can believe it exists.

—

The perimeter wall has changed since Winston drove the Mustang through it. Of course, the whole project changed. U City has grown up and evolved since.

Initially, the candidates who went with Skinner were labelled crazy. However, when reports started to come back about actual construction, the media changed the label from 'Crazy Scientist Adam Skinner' to 'Eccentric Trillionaire Adam Skinner'.

Skinner and his company became an investable commodity. *Skinner does what he says he will, regardless of how unorthodox or difficult the project is.* As the funding came, so did more media. The outside world wanted to know what this new world was like inside.

Not far from the wall, the three stop. It runs as far left and right as they can see, like a forever-train. Max sees it gets smaller in the distance, but it never shrinks completely.

The wall is 30 feet tall and ten feet thick and if they looked upon it from space, they would see a perfect square. It has been designed by the famous architect Winston Turk and has been manufactured by the APZON branch of Skinner's company brand. All Max, Alex and Thackeray see is that the perimeter wall has no beginning or end.

The scale of the construction leaves them in awe. This concrete cage has contained their lives and now their hearts race with fear-filled questions. Is this compound wall an impregnable force?

'What do you think is on the other side?' says Alex.

Neither one answers.

Max examines the structure left and right, up and down. But Alex strides on towards the wall, Thackeray following her.

Their shadows, which earlier started at their toes and ran on in front, led the way all morning. Now the darkness they followed creeps closer and closer back towards their toes to hide beneath their feet. The shadows they cast no longer know the way. Or maybe they never have. It's nearly midday.

'I need to tell you something,' says Alex, looking back to make sure Max is out of earshot. She feels nervous as she addresses Thackeray. 'It's about Max.'

She continues, searching for the right words amid Thackeray's silence.

'It's that scientist, the one who told me to get outside this wall. She was high up in the APZON building in some sort of a lab. And I saw some things.'

Those shadows, tucked completely beneath their feet, start the journey back in the direction from where they came.

'What things?'

'A lot of things ...'

Alex looks down at the tarmac as she searches for words that she doesn't have.

'I saw plants with human skin and animals with leaves. Strange creations. Spare eyes and fingernails. Tech stuff too. They are experimenting, mixing the two.'

Max is shouting behind them, so she hurries her explanations.

'They are trying to make something technological but organic-based ... maybe, and I saw an exact copy of ...'

At that moment, Max passes between them at speed.

'RRRRUUUUNNNN!'

Thackeray looks back, and begins inching away in the direction Max is running, one crab step after another as Alex stutters.

'I saw a replication of Max ... and I think Max is ...'

Thackeray places a hand on her shoulder.

'He's our friend, Alex. All that matters is that Max is our friend. Now run.'

Alex looks back to see something is swirling up dust on the horizon behind them. Whatever it is, it's coming from U City. The cloud gets bigger and bigger, spreading out and out left and right. It's getting nearer. Quickly.

All three are running hard now. Max, ahead on the road, suddenly veers off. He slides, loose stones underfoot, into the desert floor adjacent to the road. He sets off across the flat desert sand racing past the tumbleweed. Thackeray realises what his friend is heading towards and leaves the road where Max has.

Alex looks back briefly. Over her shoulder, she can see a line of snaking black SUVs, patrol trucks, coming at speed. *Skinner's APZON train of greed is in hot pursuit.* Max calls out to her. She sees him standing way off the road at the bottom of a maintenance ladder running up the perimeter wall. Max watches the line of patrol vehicles veer off the road behind Alex.

Thackeray reaches Max's side, and Max shoves him up ahead. Alex glances over her shoulder at a black tank gaining on her on the flat desert sand. Max runs back to her, incapable of doing anything else. His legs drag hers, and he shoves her up the ladder and follows. Thackeray is already calling them at the top.

'Come on! Come on!'

The first SUV skids to a stop at the base of the wall. Max makes the mistake of looking down over his shoulder and sees the young Skinner emerge from the head of the snake and more trucks pile up behind it immediately. Doors of the SUVs open and armed patrol guards spill out all over the sand.

'You never look down,' reminds Alex, feeling him pause behind her.

Max can't help remember his grandad falling back into the flames of the APZON building. He grips the ladder harder, as he thinks of friends lost and gained. He sees Alex and Thackeray above him and thinks of Nat and Conor behind him. Those memories, like bubbles floating, burst into clouds of splashing dust as a gunshot sounds below him.

—

Max opens his eyes and sees his grandad lying beside him. They are on top of one of the pumps in the forest; the one nearest their home. The old man looks with the binoculars to see if Max has hit the target. Max knows he has. Max sees himself and his grandfather fishing for plastic beside each other on the lake. He watches himself follow the old man through the trees as they head back home.

He sees the old man teaching him to drive while buried in a bunker. He teaches Max to read, swim, cook, whittle, hunt.

And Max teaches him to play chess. The old man sits on the other side of the board when thirteen-year-old Max begins placing the pieces of a game he's never seen. The chess pieces are correctly positioned, and Max holds a pawn at eye height, resting his elbow on the kitchen table.

At the table, his daughter's words are echoing in the old man's head. *This thing isn't human. Get it out of me. Stop it.* Winston recognises a truth and speaks it.

'Max, if someone creates something, especially life – that doesn't give them ownership of it. Every living thing has its own soul and has the freedom and responsibility to make its own decisions.

'You have the freedom and responsibility to live however you want. Who creates you does not own your life. Nor do they have control over it.

'You can be whatever you want to be: a machine designed for a purpose or a human free to choose. I hope I can raise you to always choose your humanity.'

Winston picks a pawn out from line of pieces and offers it to Max.

'This one's the pawn. The pawn is small. Its movement and abilities are small. It is a common piece; there are eight on each side. And what is plentiful, often becomes underappreciated and less respected. However, a pawn is not fixed to this destiny forever.'

Winston leans in closer to Max.

'If a pawn can make it to the end of the board,' says Grandad, moving a pawn to the far edge of the board closest to Max, 'then the pawn steps off the edge of the board and becomes any piece of its choosing.'

Max feels the pawn in his closed hand, but now, it feels the wrong shape. As Max looks into his reopened hand – he sees the pen. It's the pen his grandad handed him. He feels it between his hand and the side of the ladder.

Write your own ending.

'CLIMB YOU DUMMY!'

Max hears shouting from above his head and sees bullets bounce off the perimeter wall and feels the ladder rumbling in his grip. Between his legs, he sees Skinner climbing towards him from underneath taking two and three rungs at a time.

'MAX, CLIMB BEFORE I HAVE TO KICK YOUR ...'

Alex is screaming above him, so Max climbs. Alex and Thackeray reach for him at the top of the wall, pulling him onto a walkway.

Thackeray is already running to the far side of the walkway to see what is beyond this lifelong perimeter.

'You guys should really see this,' he says softly as Hitchcock reaches the top of the ladder behind them.

Hitchcock reaches over the wall and grabs Alex by the leg, flinging her back against the edge. Red lightning lines extend from his pupils as Alex struggles in his grip. Max stands perfectly still knowing he can reach them. He can get to her in time. He knows he can. He readies the pen gripped in his hand.

My whole life, my grandad has tried to get me to stop killing things by choosing my humanity, thinks Max. *Grandad never got it. I am always choosing my human side. It's the human in me that has the desire to kill.*

Max leaps forward, snatching Alex in one hand while stabbing what was Skinner's pen into the hand gripping the ladder. Skinner clutches his impaled hand in shock and stumbles backwards off the ladder. Max hears the dull thud of his body hitting the sand below. The three friends run to the far ledge and together they stand, looking out into the distance. From here, they see the world they have lived in.

Thackeray spots the camel pen and abattoir at the foot of the wall on the other side. Alex. recalls the architectural diagram hanging on the wall of the Citadel; the picture of three vast squares; three perimeter walls surrounding three compounds; three worlds. She feels smaller looking out.

Max sees the game for what it truly is: black and white pieces pitted against each other, trapped inside the square board. One female, the most dynamic, rare and valuable, yet replaceable.

Any pawn who reaches the opposition's home row (pouring blood, sweat and tears for the king) can become a queen. False promises of social mobility sold to pawns for the benefit of kings.

From kings down to pawns, the pieces have value. Their value is based on what they represent and what they represent is based on how they look. There are endless amounts of designs to distinguish each piece. Sometimes a simple line, mark, colour or pattern can illustrate the character and thus their value. Knight, rook, bishop, king, pawn, queen – we learn their value as we play, as we live. Max sees their future and what is next.

We don't know how old chess is because it has been around so long. It is possible that there are an endless number of combinations a game can take before a winner is found. The game is played in a larger cell of eight by eight smaller cells. Kings do the least and hold the most respect. The queen, a single woman among men, is the most versatile piece in the game. However, her value is overlooked by being replaceable. If a pawn reaches the far side of the board, its work is done and queen status is its reward. Pawns work the hardest, achieve the least and are so plentiful, they are disposable.

Chapter 14

Below the Surface

'ABE!'

Alex and Nat with Thackeray in tow, chase Winston back down the mountain slope.

'Winston ... I mean!'

Winston hears her but determined to get back down to the mountain valley floor, he doesn't look back.

'Winston, wait!' Alex tugs him around as she finally catches up with him.

Winston actually stops. He's intrigued by the sight of the three and secretly relieved with the rest. His old legs are no longer suited to sloped terrain.

'We're going with you. To get Max. Whatever that takes.'

Winston looks at the collection of youth.

'Why would you do that?'

Alex answers on behalf of the group.

'He's our friend.'

Winston smiles. A deep and long-held fear dissipates in him. Alex with her words and the boys' with their earnest eyes are gift-givers.

'Friends?'

Winston looks back on all the years of confinement. Was there anything different about Max at all?

—

Nat's feet land by Alex, but his attention is totally absorbed by the Mustang. Winston lifts the bonnet and Nat's disbelief turns to excitement as the old man explains the workings.

With a heave of a rope, the board covering the chamber shifts back even further. Winston knows the opening is enough to bring the Mustang up. Time is limited. Max needs their help. Thackeray and Winston begin to work overground, lowering a rope to Nat and Alex. Alex eyes are on the lantern flame in the bunker, but she helps Nat lace the rope through the car grill - back and forth to one another.

'Ok, let's do this,' says Nat standing again.

Raising his voice, he shouts back up above.

'Ok, we've tied this end.'

'On three, you push, we pull,' Winston replies. 'Alex, you get in and steer.'

Alex extinguishes the lantern, missing the warmth of the flame and the comfort it gives. When her eyes adjust, she notices the smoke-trail bend as if following a draught. *What is this?* she thinks. *How can there be a draught in the lower depths of a underground bunker?* Yet the pages on the top of the journals flicker. There's a breeze somewhere, whistling. She looks around the shelves and feels it, escaping from behind the wall.

She flicks through the stack of writing journals, but the pages are blank.

'Alex?' Nat says for the fourth time but this time louder to grasp her attention.

'Yeah?'

'I said get in and steer.'

'I don't know how to steer one of these!'

—

The Mustang breaks daylight with Alex concentrating on keeping the steering wheel straight as the others push and pull on the steel-meshed ramp. Up on the ground, Alex stays a few moments in the silence of the car. By the time she gets out, Nat and Thackeray are helping Winston replace the board cover over the bunker. Alex is the last to emerge from the space.

When the board conceals the bunker from sight again, another draught fills the bunker. It whispers around the space occupied by the Mustang. The journal on top of the pile of books flaps in the wind, and the cover flips open. It knocks the lamp, which topples over on the old man's writing desk.

The fallen lantern rolls on the table beside Sarah's stacked journals. The hidden ink on the open page lies in the darkness for no one to read. The words are concealed in the bunker guarded by the giant knight.

Winston would never sit here to write again. Nor would he need to dig again. The wind blows a final membrane of dirt wall forward. And with that wind, the escape route to the tunnels and to the other compounds and the others is revealed.

A desert's distance away, Alex finally knows what to do next. They must go back in.

—

After each turn, the options for the next move increases exponentially. To begin with, there are an average of 400 potential placements. This quickly escalates to 318 billion after only four turns. How many combinations and patterns can a game take?

Once the first move is made, the clock starts.

Epilogue: Black or White

White stars in a black night sky and black inked words on a white page. Without the darkness of space, the stars could not twinkle light, and the absence of the starlight gifts us black velvet night. Dark is the absence of light. Light is the absence of darkness.

Identical opposites and forever reliant on each other for their own existence.

Gliding endlessly in space through these planes of opposites, like a Möbius strip through which we fall. A strip of fabric, one side Space and the other Time. One way is falling. Every point along the strips unique in its placement. Places, times, touching back-to-back, twisting around us. Space and Time come together and crystalise like a snowflake, every one unique.

A snowflake from thin air in Space. A white star in a black night sky. Black ink splashing on the whiteness of a page.

Twenty-six letters, one million words, 7,000 languages. The number of ways in which these can combine is as unique as snowflakes. So many combinations, formed from thin air, a strip of letters, a strip of time, a strip of places, a story.

Letters on the page, black and white. Life is simple, one

thing or another, choices. Yes or no, on or off, go or stay, night or day, light or dark, black or white.

Your choices will cut a groove into existence, and the pattern those grooves draw is how you will be remembered. Paint your picture.

Additional Reading

B.F Skinner's Pigeon Box
M. Turk Chess Machine
Plato's Cave
Camel Through the Eye of a Needle

Please Review

Dear reader,
If you enjoyed this book would you kindly spread the word or leave a review online so other readers who enjoy this type of story will find it more easily. Your feedback will make all the difference in getting word out about this book. Thank you in advance.

D.S Cash
Instagram - @ds_cash_writes